m

STORMY VOWS

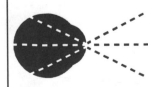

STORMY VOWS

IRIS JOHANSEN

THORNDIKE PRESS
A part of Gale, Cengage Learning

Detroit • New York • San Francisco • New Haven, Conn • Waterville, Maine • London

GALE
CENGAGE Learning"

LIBRARY OF CONGRESS CATALOGING-IN-PUBLICATION DATA

Johansen, Iris.
   Stormy vows / by Iris Johansen.
      p. cm. — (Thorndike Press large print famous authors)
   ISBN-13: 978-1-4104-1053-5 (hardcover : alk. paper)
   ISBN-10: 1-4104-1053-6 (hardcover : alk. paper)
   1. Motion picture actors and actresses—Fiction. 2. Large type books. I. Title.
   PS3560.O275S76 2009
   813'.54—dc22
                                     2008041341

Published in 2009 by arrangement with The Bantam Dell Publishing Group, a division of Random House, Inc.

Printed in the United States of America
1 2 3 4 5 6 7 12 11 10 09 08

STORMY VOWS

ONE

Brenna Sloan turned slowly in front of the mirror appraising her reflection with critical eyes. A frown creased her forehead and she chewed her lower lip. The simple black wool skirt and white silk blouse had seemed an understated yet chic ensemble when she had chosen it twenty minutes ago, but now she was having second thoughts. Was it perhaps too understated? She definitely wanted to make an impression in what might be the most important interview of her career.

She shrugged and turned away with a sigh. It would just have to do. Her wardrobe wasn't that extensive anyway. She quickly gathered her suede jacket and purse and hurried into the living room.

A chubby golden-haired two-year-old cherub looked up at her from the center of a fiberglass playpen and smiled amiably. He pulled himself up on sturdy legs, looking absurdly adorable in his blue corduroy pants and a T-shirt with LOS ANGELES DODGERS emblazoned across the front.

"We go, Mama?" he asked contentedly. Randy always wanted to go, Brenna thought wryly. For him, every trip was a pleasant adventure, and he certainly had enough of them.

She swung him out of the playpen, planting a kiss on his satin cheek and gathering him close for a quick hug.

"We go," she affirmed. She put him down on the floor while she folded the collapsible playpen, then picked up a canvas bag of toys that was always kept handy. He watched her serenely, familiar with the ritual that was repeated sometimes twice or three times a day.

Tucking the playpen under her arm, she gathered her jacket, purse, and the toy carryall and headed for the door. Randy toddled beside her happily as they left the apartment and crossed to the elevator.

"Mama carry?" he asked. That, too, was part of the ritual. He really didn't expect it, but he tried every time just the same, Brenna thought tenderly.

"No, Randy must walk," Brenna said firmly, as the door to the self-service elevator opened and they entered the small shabby cubicle. The apartment building was

8

only two stories and an elevator was not really necessary, but she blessed it fervently each time she took Randy out. Loaded like a pack horse, as she usually was, she never would have made it without a major catastrophe if she had had to help Randy down the stairs. Besides, Randy loved elevators. It was another magic adventure for him — not as intriguing as the fascinating escalators in the department stores, but interesting all the same.

The elevator door opened, and she shepherded Randy out and down the hall to the manager's apartment. Randy knew the way well and nodded with satisfaction as they paused before the door.

"Auntie Viv," he said placidly, knowing that behind the door was another disciple who provided toys, cookies, and caresses.

"Yes, sweetheart," Brenna said. "She's going to watch you while mama goes out." She rang the bell.

"Come in, Brenna," Vivian Barlow called, and when Brenna and Randy entered, she waved a freshly manicured hand from where she was sitting on an early American couch, applying a coat of clear gloss to her nails. "Sorry, love," she said with an absent smile. "I know you're in a bit of a hurry, but would you mind getting Randy settled before you leave. I have a photography session later on this afternoon, and my polish isn't dry yet."

"Another dishwashing detergent commercial?" Brenna asked, as she unfolded the collapsible playpen and set it up swiftly.

Vivian Barlow nodded her sleekly coiffed gray head. "Yep," she drawled with eyebrows raised wryly. "One of those comparison jobs, where the granddaughter loses to grandma in the beautiful hands sweepstakes." She simpered coyly. "And all because I've washed my china all my born days with antiscum."

"Antiscum!" Brenna laughed.

"Well, it's something like that," Vivian said vaguely. She got briskly to her feet, strolled over to where Randy was sitting on the floor, and kissed him on the top of his head. "How are you, slugger?" she asked fondly. She was an ardent baseball fan, and it was she who had gifted Randy with the Dodger T-shirt. In her early sixties, Vivian Barlow was attractive, well dressed, and beautifully preserved. She also had the warmest smile and the most humorous gray eyes Brenna had ever seen.

A short time after she had become friends with her ultramodern landlady, Brenna had learned that Vivian had been divorced twice and widowed once. In a moment of confi-

10

dence Vivian had confessed wistfully, "I've always been afraid of missing something along the way, so I reach out and grab." She'd made a face. "I've made some pretty dumb grabs in my time." Vivian had been an actress all her adult life, playing bit parts and walk-ons in hundreds of films and stage productions. When husband number three died and left her a small apartment complex and an adequate income, she had retired, only to find herself completely bored. It wasn't long before she discovered the perfect outlet for her energy in the world of television commercials. She was much in demand these days in the role of the modern older woman who was the antithesis of the crochety granny figures of the past.

"I still think you'd be perfect for shampoo and soap commercials," Vivian said critically. "You have a certain dryad look. It's as though you grew up in some forest glade."

She looked appraisingly at Brenna who was putting Randy's favorite toys in the playpen before lifting him into the center of the mat. Brenna straightened and a grin lit up her face with breathtaking poignancy.

"The John Harris Memorial Home was not precisely a sylvan glade," she said dryly. On the contrary, the orphanage where she had grown up had no time for such foolishness as nymphs and dryads, she thought wistfully.

Vivian looked up sharply, but made no comment.

"You're quite dressed up today," she said.

Brenna didn't look at her as she gathered up her jacket and purse. "I have an audition," she said, almost beneath her breath.

"An audition? Why didn't you tell me?" Vivian asked delightedly. "Where is it? Tell me all about it."

"There isn't much to tell," Brenna said with feigned casualness. "Charles arranged for me to try out for a part in a picture a former pupil of his is producing. It probably won't come to anything."

"I didn't know that Charles had any contacts in films," Vivian said speculatively. "Who is it?"

Brenna drew a deep breath and turned to look at her friend, revealing the tenseness in her face. "Michael Donovan."

Vivian's brows shot up, and she gave a low soundless whistle. "Michael Donovan! What a break for you."

Everyone in films knew of Michael Donovan. Only in his late thirties, he was already a legend. He had shot across the Hollywood firmament like a fiery comet. He was a writer-director without equal, and had recently turned to producing his own films with similar success. He had directed three of the biggest money-making films of all time, and as he had put up the money for two of them, he had become a multimillionaire from the proceeds. He had invested a portion of that wealth in his own film colony in southern Oregon, where he had gathered the best talents in film-making. His image had grown to such proportions that even his name gave off a Midas-like glitter.

Brenna shrugged. "It's only an audition. I'm to read for the casting director, Josh Hernandez." Her composure cracked, and she closed her eyes and took a deep breath. "Oh, Vivian, I'm so nervous."

Vivian patted her on the shoulder. "You'll do just fine," she said bracingly. "You're good, Brenna, really good."

"There are hundreds of talented actresses in this town," Brenna said gloomily. "And most of them are out of work."

Vivian nodded sympathetically. "It's a competitive business," she said. "I doubt you would even make it past the first receptionist at Donovan's casting office without a personal introduction. I had no idea Charles knew Michael Donovan."

"Neither did I," Brenna replied. "I don't

think he wanted to trade on the association. That's why it's so important that I do well at the reading. I can't let him down after he went to the trouble of asking for a special favor from Mr. Donovan."

She moistened her lips nervously, and then straightened her shoulders. "Well, they can only turn me down," she said with bravado. She flashed a quick smile at the older woman. "Wish me luck?"

"Break a leg, Brenna," Vivian said.

Giving a quick kiss on the top of Randy's silky head, Brenna left.

It was only as she was maneuvering her ancient gray Honda out of the apartment complex parking lot that she allowed her thoughts to turn back to the interview ahead.

When Charles had told her what he had arranged for her and handed her the script for *Wild Heritage,* she had been stunned. Never in her wildest dreams had she imagined a chance to audition for Donovan. Charles had been almost childishly pleased at her surprise. He explained gruffly that Donovan had been a student of his quite some years before and they still kept in casual contact.

"When I read that Michael had bought the book *Wild Heritage,* I knew you'd be perfect for Angie," he said simply. He patted her on the shoulder awkwardly. "Do me proud, Brenna."

Wild Heritage centered around the character of Angie Linden, a complex young woman struggling to overcome her promiscuous past. It had everything: pathos, humor, and an underlying hint of tragedy. Any actress would give her eyeteeth for the role, and Brenna was frankly skeptical of such a plum being awarded to an unknown. If Charles Wilkes had not been so insistent, she wouldn't have even consented to go for the reading. But she could not disappoint him after all he had done for her.

The address Charles had given her was in downtown Los Angeles, and when she located it, she was surprised to find it was a modest two-story brick building with a discreet plaque reading DONOVAN ENTERPRISES LTD. Rather an unimposing establishment for a man of Donovan's reputed flamboyance, she thought, as she parked in front of the building. After putting coins in the meter, she entered the swinging glass doors. A smiling receptionist directed her to Studio B on the second floor.

Studio B was actually a small theater with a raised stage and several rows of padded velvet seats. Two seats near the door were occupied by a short, dark-haired man in his thirties and a casually dressed red-haired woman of about her own age. The man rose to his feet as she entered, picking up a clipboard from the seat next to him.

"Miss Sloan?" His smile was quick, charging his thin, clever face with warmth. "Josh Hernandez, and this is my assistant, Billie Perkins." The red-haired woman smiled in acknowledgment of Brenna's nod. "It's a pleasure to meet you."

Brenna relaxed slightly, and drew a deep breath of relief. Perhaps it wouldn't be so bad after all. Josh Hernandez was far from the cigar-smoking, beady-eyed executive of her nervous imagination.

A smile lit her face, and Josh Hernandez caught his breath involuntarily. God, he hadn't seen a smile like that since Audrey Hepburn.

"I'm very happy to meet you, Mr. Hernandez," she said shyly. Then looking around the tiny theater, "This isn't at all what I expected."

He grinned and shrugged. "If you get through this intact, you still have to take a screen test. But Mr. Donovan prefers that the first audition take place here. He thinks the stage highlights the actor, and lets us better appraise the body movements."

"Mr. Donovan appears to be a man of original ideas," Brenna said lightly.

"He is indeed, Miss Sloan," Josh Hernandez said ruefully. "He is indeed." He looked down at the clipboard and detached a form. "If you will fill this out, we'll get on with the actual audition."

The audition form was quite short, and in a few minutes she had completed it and returned it to Hernandez.

He gestured to the stage casually. "When you're ready," he said easily.

Brenna mounted the four steps at the side of the stage, and moved to center stage. Drawing a deep breath to still the quivering butterflies, she asked quietly, "Where do you want me to begin?"

"Start with Angie's monologue on page three, scene two," Hernandez said. "Billie will read Joe."

Brenna began to read, and, as usual, once she became involved with the character, she forgot everything else. All nervous apprehension vanished in her absorption with Angie Linden. She actually began to enjoy herself, and was almost disappointed when Hernandez called a halt to the reading. She knew with a confident thrill that it had been a good audition. She had done well.

Hernandez came up the stairs two at a

time, a broad grin on his dark face. "A really great job, Miss Sloan!"

She looked up at him hopefully, her face glowing. "You like it?" she asked breathlessly. Hernandez stared down into her face bemusedly. "Damn, if you photograph well, you'll be a natural." Then he added quickly, "The final decision isn't mine, of course. But if I have anything to say about it, you have the role."

"Hold it, Josh!"

They both looked with startled eyes toward the door.

The red-haired man leaning indolently against the doorjamb was dressed casually in faded jeans and a cream-colored shirt with sleeves rolled to the elbow. Despite the casualness of his dress, there was no mistaking his identity. Though Michael Donovan was militantly vigilant of his privacy, he was excellent copy, and newspaper photos of him appeared on occasion. Once seen, he couldn't be forgotten.

Brenna's breath caught in her throat at the explosive impact of the man. He was not at all handsome, she thought dazedly, and then was amazed that she had noticed because Michael Donovan made conventional observations unimportant. His blunt, rough-hewn features carried a power all their own, and the piercing blue of his eyes cut through what wasn't essential with the force of a lightning bolt. The air around him seemed to crackle with the strength and vitality of his personality. The mahogany hair and eyebrows, and the tall muscular body were dwarfed by the sheer overpowering virility that emanated from the man.

He moved with lithe swiftness past a dazzled Billie Perkins, to mount the steps and cross to stand before Brenna and Hernandez.

At close range, he was even more intimidating, and Brenna stepped back instinctively, a fact that Donovan noted with narrowed eyes. His mouth twisted cynically as he turned to Hernandez. "I believe you're slipping, Josh," he said smoothly. "It's not like you to make even a tentative commitment without consulting me. Isn't your usual policy, Don't call us, we'll call you?" His eyes traveled intimately from the top of Brenna's glossy head to the delicate bones of her ankles. "It would take something pretty world-shaking to budge you from your standard procedure."

Hernandez was looking at Donovan with dark, puzzled eyes. "There was no commitment, Mr. Donovan," he said quietly. "I do plead guilty to enthusiasm. She gave a damn good reading."

Donovan nodded casually. "She was good, I caught the last half."

Brenna's eyes brightened as they flew to Donovan's face. His gaze had never left her expressive face, and he caught the look of eager expectancy radiating from her. He said briskly, "There's no use raising your hopes, Miss Sloan. You won't do for the role."

The soft doe eyes widened with shock at the cruel bluntness of his statement. "But why?" she asked in bewilderment. "You said I was good."

Donovan had taken the clipboard from Hernandez and was swiftly perusing the information on the personnel sheet. "You were good," he said coolly. "That doesn't mean you are suited for the role of Angie. Any number of actresses could have given an equally convincing reading."

Hernandez opened his mouth as if to protest, but, at a lightning glance from Donovan, he subsided with a shrug.

Donovan continued, "What we need for Angie is someone with more experience."

"Professional experience?" Brenna asked, thinking she understood. Though Donovan didn't have the reputation of playing it safe by hiring box office draws, it was logical that he would not want to gamble a multimillion-dollar movie on an unknown.

But Donovan was shaking his head. "I don't give a damn about professional experience," he said swiftly. "I'm talking about personal experience. You gave a nice surface reading, but I want more than that for Angie. I want the actress who plays the part to reach down and bring up real gut feelings." He gestured toward the clipboard in his hand. "You're only twenty, and you've had no formal theatrical training, so perhaps you're unfamiliar with Stanislavski and sense memory?"

"Stanislavski? Method acting?" she asked dazedly.

"Precisely. I forgot for a moment that you are a protégée of Wilkes'. You're aware that method acting endorses using your own emotions and experiences as the basis for your performance. Angie Linden is a woman who has lived life to the fullest, despite her youth. She's had lovers by the score, and has suffered disillusionment and cruelty." His eyes lingered on her face. "You look as if you still have the morning dew on you, Miss Sloan," he said. "Angie Linden is definitely midnight lace and French perfume."

Brenna could feel a slow anger beginning

21

to build. "Let me understand you, Mr. Donovan," she said carefully. "It's not because I'm not a good enough actress to play the part. You're refusing to give me the role because I don't have a torrid past to draw on for Angie's character?"

His vivid blue eyes were curiously watchful. "That's quite right," he said silkily. "I'm sure you would do very well in ingenue or Juliet roles, Miss Sloan."

"That's the most ridiculous thing I've ever heard in my life," she said flatly, ignoring Hernandez' hastily drawn breath at her insolence. Her anger had leaped to full blaze, and the usual limpid brown eyes were sparkling with feeling. In just a few minutes, she had been moved from hope to bewilderment to disappointment by this arrogant dictator, and now he was denying her a chance that might mean her whole future . . . and denying it on the flimsiest pretext imaginable!

"You think so?" Donovan asked idly, his eyes still observing her as if she were an interesting new specimen at the zoo. "I take it you don't agree with Stanislavski, Miss Sloan?"

"An actress can work with any number of tools that help her perfect a characterization. Theories, like method acting and sense memory, are just that — tools. But they are far from the only tools, if you're to be any good at all. A creative imagination, sensitivity, and just plain hard work are much more important. To subscribe so fanatically to one aspect of a complex whole is utterly absurd." She tossed her hair back from her face, and said emphatically, "To deny me the part because you think I lack sex appeal is totally and completely asinine."

Donovan's eyes were amused as they moved over her lazily, causing a flood of heat to envelope her body. "I never said you lacked sex appeal. Merely experience." Blue devils gleamed in his eyes as he continued softly. "A lack that I would be more than happy to supply."

She could feel the blood rush to her face in a burning blush that was due as much to anger as embarrassment. The knowledge that he was toying with her increased her rage. Donovan's affairs were legion. He was reputedly as sexually active as a tomcat, and with some of the most sophisticated and beautiful women in the world, if the gossip columns were correct. The possibility that he would find a twenty-year-old "ingenue-type" attractive was ludicrous. No, he was merely revenging himself for the insults she had hurled at him by teasing her as a cat would a mouse.

"I don't deserve that," she said quietly, lifting her chin defiantly. "I know you're annoyed with me, but don't descend to that sexist casting couch routine to put me in my place, Mr. Donovan. I have a valid argument and I'm sorry you're too blind and pigheaded to appreciate it." She turned and stalked majestically off the stage, leaving the two men staring after her. She paused at the door, and turned to meet Donovan's narrowed eyes. "You're wrong, Michael Donovan," she said with serene conviction. "I could have made something very special out of Angie Linden." Her mouth twisted wryly. "And if my memory serves, Juliet was a very sexy lady," she said softly. "So you're wrong there, too." She strode from the theater.

Two

A white core of anger burned like a piece of molten steel in Brenna as she went through the motions of driving home, picking up Randy from Vivian's, and taking him back to their apartment. Once home, Brenna put Randy down for his afternoon nap. She scrupulously removed all the toys from his bed, knowing that if there was even one distraction, Randy would find it and refuse to go to sleep. She ignored his pleading eyes, turned him over on his stomach, tucked his blanket around him and, patted his round bottom. "Sleep," she said firmly, and closed the door decisively behind her.

She leaned wearily against the door, feeling as if the violent emotions of the morning had savaged her and left her weak and drained. She moved slowly to the couch, and curled up in the corner, leaning her head on the arm. Unexpectedly a drop of moisture coursed down her cheek, and she brushed it aside angrily. Tears? No, dammit, she wouldn't cry. She wouldn't give Michael Donovan the satisfaction of upsetting her that much. She was tougher than that. Hadn't Janine said that, she thought suddenly, her throat tightening. She could remember her sister kneeling beside her bed, her ash-blond hair wild around her white face, tears streaming down her cheeks. "You're strong, Brenna," Janine had gasped. "You've always been stronger than me, even though I'm older. Help me, Brenna. Help me!"

Brenna shook her head, her eyes filling helplessly at the poignant memory. "Damn you, Michael Donovan," she whispered huskily, her hands balling into fists. Usually she could keep the memories at bay with her customary determination, blocking out the still raw emotions that had torn her apart and left her defenseless in their aftermath. Now they came flooding back, tumbling over each other in a chaotic eruption brought on by her distressing experience with Donovan.

Janine had been right: Brenna had always been tougher than her older sister, though heaven knows how much was integral, and how much a result of her upbringing in the orphanage that had been the only home they had known since Brenna was four and Janine eight. Their father had deserted their mother shortly after Brenna was born, and, as their mother had had to work long hours to support the three of them, she had not had the time to give her younger child the love and attention she had lavished on Janine. Consequently, when their mother died of pneumonia shortly after Brenna's fourth birthday, Brenna was not as devastated as she might have been. Janine, on the other hand, had been struck down by the second catastrophic blow of her young life, and she never quite recovered. They had been sent to the John Harris Memorial Home when an investigation by the welfare department had uncovered no relatives. Brenna had adjusted quickly to her new circumstances, but Janine had retreated behind a wall of shyness, developing a finely balanced sensitivity that shut away the present, letting in only the familiar figures of the past. Always an imaginative child, she lived in a world of her own making, and clung to Brenna with an almost fanatic need and devotion.

When she had been released from the home at seventeen, Janine had obtained a secretarial position at Chadeaux Wineries in Los Angeles. She had worked hard, and soon had been promoted to the executive offices. When she rented her own apartment, she persuaded the home to release fifteen-year-old Brenna in her custody. Brenna had been as happy as Janine at the move. Though not dependent on her sister for affection, she loved the fragile Janine with a deep, fierce protectiveness that was a result of fighting a hundred battles in her defense with the other children at the home.

That first year had been full of contentment and independence, with Brenna continuing her education at a local high school and becoming increasingly involved in drama classes and high school plays. Absorbed with her first taste of the exhilarating art of acting, she had not noticed, at first, Janine's own infatuation with Paul Chadeaux, the heir apparent to the Chadeaux Wineries. She had met the sleek blond young man when he had picked up Janine for dates, but he had not really registered other than causing her to wonder absently what on earth Janine saw in him. Then, with a knowledge beyond her years, Brenna realized he had an assurance that would inevitably attract an insecure girl like Janine. His aura could be obtained only from growing up with money, the right schools, and a solid family background.

Janine continued to see Paul Chadeaux,

and Brenna noted the transformation that manifested itself in her delicate sister. Janine glowed with an almost incandescent radiance, hopelessly infatuated with the man. When that realization came home to her, Brenna began to watch Chadeaux with critical eyes and what she saw filled her with alarm. Paul Chadeaux treated her sister with a selfish unconcern that made Brenna react with fierce indignation. He broke dates without notice, and often spoke to Janine with such impatient cruelty that Brenna wanted to wring his neck. She knew better than to speak to Janine. Paul could do no wrong in her eyes. So she watched helplessly while Janine continued blindly on her path to destruction.

Janine was almost three months pregnant when she confided in Brenna. She had been childishly happy, as she prepared to go out that night with Chadeaux. Brenna's face had whitened with shock when Janine confessed quite simply that she was pregnant with Chadeaux's child. Brenna had been doing her homework on one of the twin beds, idly watching as Janine put on her makeup at the vanity. Janine had dropped the information into the conversation almost casually.

"Does he know?" Brenna asked numbly.

A secret smile curved Janine's mouth as she brushed her hair slowly. "Not yet," she said dreamily. "I've just found out for sure today. But he'll be glad. I know he will. It'll just mean we'll be married sooner than we expected."

"He's asked you to marry him?" Brenna asked with relief. Perhaps Chadeaux wasn't the swine she suspected.

"Of course he has," Janine said serenely. "There are just some minor problems with his family. Paul's just been waiting for the right time to tell them."

"How long have you been engaged?" Brenna asked grimly.

"About four months," Janine said vaguely, her eyes taking on a glow that lit up her delicate features. "A baby, Brenna!" she said breathlessly. "I've always wanted someone of my very own, and now I'm going to have a husband and a baby. It seems too good to be true."

It seemed too good to be true to Brenna, also, but she couldn't puncture the lovely dream world that her sister was living in. "That's wonderful, Janine," she said gently.

"I'm going to tell Paul tonight," Janine said eagerly. "I can hardly wait."

Brenna watched her leave that night with the feeling of helplessness that had plagued her sharpened to a positive dread.

Janine had awakened her in the early hours of the morning, her face a mask of suffering, almost hysterical with grief, pleading with Brenna to help her.

"I was wrong, Brenna," Janine had sobbed. "He doesn't care anything about me." Her eyes were wide, as if she were in shock. "He wants to kill my baby. He wants me to get an abortion."

Brenna had cradled Janine's slender body, and rocked her in an agony of sympathy. "It'll be all right, honey," she had whispered huskily.

"He doesn't want to see me anymore," Janine had cried, her eyes wild. "He said I was a stupid fool not to protect myself. He said if I caused any trouble, he'd say the baby wasn't his . . . that I should get rid of 'the little bastard.' " She shuddered convulsively.

Brenna felt a rage so terrible, that if Chadeaux had been in the room she would have killed him. "Forget him, Janine," she'd said fiercely. "He's not worth another thought."

"He's so evil," Janine had said with childlike wonder, "I've never known anyone so evil. He wants to kill my baby. I can't let him do that, Brenna."

"No, I know you can't, honey," she'd said slowly, a chill running through her at the pathetic expression on Janine's face. Always balanced on the thin edge of reality, had this blow been too much for her? "We'll work something out. I promise you. Why don't you go to bed now?"

Janine rose obediently to her feet. "You're so strong, Brenna. You'll help me keep my baby."

In the following months, the thought of the child growing inside her seemed to be the only thing that kept Janine from a complete breakdown. It would have been impossible for her to continue at Chadeaux Wineries, so Brenna insisted that Janine quit her job, and let Brenna assume the burden of responsibility for both of them. Janine obeyed with the docility of a child, and didn't even object when Brenna dropped out of school, and took a job in a neighborhood pharmacy. Brenna had some clerical skills that probably would have paid better, but it would have meant searching further afield for a job and leaving Janine alone too long.

Janine's obsession that Paul would harm her child continued. No amount of gentle persuasion on Brenna's part could convince her that Chadeaux would not suddenly appear and take the child away from her.

It was only after receiving a bill from the prenatal clinic in Janine's eighth month of pregnancy that Brenna realized the full extent of her sister's fear. The bill was for services to Brenna Sloan *not* Janine Sloan. When confronted with the bill, Janine had smiled tranquilly. "I had to do it, Brenna," she'd said calmly. "It's the only way to protect my baby. I've thought it all out. I've been very clever."

"What have you done, Janine?" Brenna had asked tiredly. "Why is my name on this bill?"

Janine had leaned forward and whispered confidentially, "Don't you see, we're going to pretend the baby is yours. Then Paul will have no legal right to the baby. It'll be your name on the birth certificate as the mother, not mine."

"Janine, it won't work," Brenna had said hopelessly, knowing her protests would do no good.

"Of course it will," Janine had insisted serenely. "You'll see, Brenna. Everyone will think the baby's yours." Her eyes clouded. "But the baby will really be mine, you know," she had said jealously. "It's just pretend, like when we were children. You won't try to take my child away from me too?"

Tears had closed her throat as Brenna leaned forward to stroke her sister's thin cheek. "No, it will be just pretend, Love," she'd said huskily.

Janine had never lived to enjoy her baby. Three days after giving birth to Randy, she had died of complications.

An indignant yell caused Brenna to sit bolt upright on the couch, dabbing quickly at her eyes. She was on her feet and into the other room with lithe swiftness. Randy broke off a yell and stretched out his arms invitingly. "Mama carry?" he wheedled, smiling angelically.

"Some nap, young man," Brenna said sternly. She lifted him from the bed and held him close for a brief moment. He felt so good.

"Too tight, Mama," he protested, wriggling vigorously.

In the two years since Janine's death she had never tried to deny the natural assumption that she was Randy's mother. Somehow she had felt that she owed it to Janine that Randy have a real mother of his own, not just a loving aunt. The only people she cared about, Vivian Barlow and Charles Wilkes, had tactfully avoided probing her relationship with Randy. As for the others, she couldn't care less what they thought. It had not taken her long to find that the suggestion that she was an unwed mother still carried a stigma even in these "liberal" times. Brenna's mouth curved bitterly. After two years of being looked upon as a fallen woman, it was ironic that she should lose her greatest career opportunity to date because Donovan had judged her to be too innocent.

Charles Wilkes was getting out of his Volkswagon Rabbit when she pulled into the parking lot at the rear of the theater that evening. He smiled broadly and waved, as she parked in the spot next to him and turned off the ignition.

In his late fifties, Wilkes looked older than his years. His snow-white hair, gray-white beard, and rotund figure made him look like an intellectual Santa Claus. This look was augmented by the gray tweed suit and horn-rimmed glasses perched on his nose.

He was beside her in a moment, and took the sleeping Randy from her as she opened the door of the Honda. He handled the baby with practiced ease, wrapping the blanket more tightly around the small body.

He stood there, his face as eager as a child's.

"How did it go?" he whispered over Randy's head.

She made a face, as she opened the rear door and pulled out Randy's playpen. "It was a complete disaster," she said gloomily. "The *Titanic* was a success story in comparison."

Profound disappointment flooded Wilkes' face. "Hernandez didn't like your reading?" he asked, as they walked toward the stage door.

"Mr. Hernandez liked it," Brenna said caustically. "It was your old pupil that found me wanting."

"Michael was there?" Charles asked incredulously, a pleased smile on his face. "It was kind of him to give the audition his personal attention."

"I assure you I would have been a thousand times more fortunate if he hadn't been so 'kind.' " Brenna bit her lip, then confessed miserably, "I'm sorry, Charles. I let you down. I not only fouled up my chance of a part, but I lost my temper with Mr. Donovan."

A grin creased his face, making him look more cherubic than ever. "Don't worry, Brenna," he said genially. "I imagine it was an interesting experience for Michael. He's so used to being kowtowed to these days, it must have been quite refreshing to have someone stand up to him."

"I'm glad you think so," Brenna said dryly. "Somehow I don't think he felt the same way."

They had reached the backstage door and Charles deftly balanced Randy on one arm while he held the heavy metal door open for Brenna.

The Rialto was actually an old renovated movie house, one of many small neighborhood theaters that had closed after the advent of television. It had remained a boarded-up derelict until Wilkes joyously discovered it among the property listings of a small real estate company. With boundless enthusiasm, he had enlisted the aid of the students of his classes at the university to make the theater a habitable home for his own community theater. Brenna had learned later that Charles had been amazingly fortunate in his find. Los Angeles was the possessor of innumerable amateur theater groups looking for a showcase for their talents in the optimistic hope that one magic night a talent scout or agent would discover them. Shabby and antiquated as the Rialto was, it had become dearly familiar to Brenna in the last two years.

The play they were rehearsing now was an original work of one of Charles' more talented students. Brenna's role was small but important to the production. After playing the lead in the last play, she was enjoying the lighter responsibility that was hers in this charming romantic comedy.

That is, she would have enjoyed it, but for the scene she was forced to do with Blake Conroy. The scene would have been a relatively simple one if she had not had to contend with Conroy's sophomoric shenanigans. In her less irritable moments she could see why Charles had chosen Conroy for the romantic lead. He was an adequate actor, and he certainly looked the part. His bronze curly hair and tall muscular body, together with a rather dashing moustache, made him look as if he had just stepped out of a cigarette commercial. In all truth, he had done just that. He had been a popular and well-paid model before an enterprising theatrical agent convinced him that he was wasted in magazines, and his true métier was stage and screen. He must have been extremely easy to persuade for Brenna found him to be the most egotistical and smugly self-satisfied man she had ever met. Added to that, he was convinced that he was God's gift to women, and spent a good portion of every romantic scene attempting to fondle any available portion of her anatomy that came under his rather moist, fumbling hands.

Tonight was no exception, and when she had unobtrusively moved his hand from her buttocks to her waist for the third time, she was tempted to dig her nails into his well-manicured hand. With some difficulty, she managed to finish the scene and walked into the wings followed closely by Conroy.

When she was far enough from the stage to avoid disturbing the action, she whirled and faced Conroy. Her blazing eyes caused his smug smile to fade. "I've warned you before, Blake," she said tightly. "I won't be handled by you. You either keep your hands to yourself or I'll put some marks on that pretty face of yours." She curved her hand into a claw to demonstrate her sincerity.

A flicker of unease passed over Conroy's face, before his inherent conceit discounted her threat. "I like a girl with spirit," he said smugly, reaching out a hand to cup her shoulder.

A line straight out of a John Wayne movie, she thought with exasperation, slapping his hand aside. "You'll see a violent demonstration of my 'spirit' if you don't listen to me,

Blake," she said grimly. "I mean what I say."

"You don't have to pretend with me, Brenna," he said confidently, taking a step closer. "I know what a hot little number like you needs. Why don't I drive you home after rehearsal? You live alone, don't you?"

"No, I don't live alone," she said through her teeth. "I live with my son."

"Oh, the kid." Conroy shrugged. "We'll just tuck him into bed." An intimate smile curved his mouth. "And then I'll tuck you into bed."

"I'm afraid Miss Sloan will be too busy to accommodate you tonight, Conroy."

Brenna froze with shock as she turned to see Michael Donovan strolling casually toward them. He was dressed in a navy blue shirt and slacks and should not have been impressive, but to Brenna's annoyance, he seemed to make his surroundings shrink, as if he were draining their identity from them. Certainly, Blake Conroy became insipid in comparison.

"What are you doing here, Mr. Donovan?" she asked bitterly. "Slumming?"

"We didn't finish our chat this morning, Miss Sloan," Donovan said coolly. "I dislike leaving loose ends."

"I thought we both made our positions quite clear," Brenna replied. "I know I did."

Conroy was listening to the exchange with increasing irritation. He never liked losing the limelight, particularly when he was smugly certain he was making headway. "Can't you see the lady isn't interested?" he drawled. "Why don't you go away?"

Donovan gave him a razor sharp glance that appraised and then dismissed him as though he didn't exist.

"Where can we go to talk?" he asked Brenna tersely. "Charles said you were through for the night. Why don't I take you out for a drink?"

"Now, see here," Conroy protested, moving a step closer to Brenna and taking her arm. "Brenna and I were about to leave."

"I heard," Donovan said shortly. "Something about tucking her into bed, wasn't it?" He smiled mirthlessly. "Forget it, Conroy. In fact, it might be a good idea if you forget about Miss Sloan entirely. She won't have time for you anymore."

"She'll be too busy with you, I suppose," Conroy said sarcastically.

"Right." Donovan nodded, his eyes amused. "You might say, I intend to fully occupy Miss Sloan from now on."

Even Conroy wasn't too dense to catch the double-entendre in Donovan's statement. An ugly sneer twisted his face as he glanced at Brenna's scarlet cheeks. "That's up to the lady, isn't it? Brenna doesn't seem too eager to take you up on your offer." His hand caressed her arm. "How about it, beautiful?"

Brenna gritted her teeth in exasperation. She was tempted to use Conroy as a bulwark against the domineering tactics of Michael Donovan. Yet she knew if she offered any encouragement to Blake, he would make himself more obnoxious than ever.

"Oh, go away, Blake!" she said wearily, running her fingers through her hair.

Donovan chuckled. Reaching out, he took Conroy's hand from Brenna's arm and pulled her closer to his side. She shot him a glance of acute dislike that he ignored urbanely. "Yes, do go away, Blake," he repeated mildly.

Conroy gave a smothered curse, and his look at Brenna was positively lethal. He stalked off, every line of his body expressing his outrage.

"That's the best acting he's done tonight," Donovan said idly.

"You were watching?" Brenna asked, surprised.

Donovan nodded. "I wanted to talk to Charles," he said. "And I wanted to see you perform again. Two birds with one stone, so to speak."

Brenna looked at him skeptically. "You came to see me?" she questioned doubtfully. "That's rather hard to believe."

"I'm a busy man, Miss Sloan," he said curtly. "I don't have time to play games. Now, how about that drink?"

She shook her head wearily. "It's been a long day, Mr. Donovan, and I'm tired." She met his eyes steadily, and for a brief moment lost the thread of what she wanted to say as she was caught up by the sheer magnetism of the man. She took a deep breath and forced herself to look away. "You see, I'm afraid I don't believe you," she said defiantly. "I think you do enjoy playing games. We both know you gave Blake Conroy a completely wrong impression for some reason of your own. You couldn't possibly be interested in me. I'm not your type."

Donovan cocked one eyebrow, his blue eyes narrowed. "Please go on, Miss Sloan," he drawled softly. "I'd be delighted to discover what you judge to be my type of woman."

She shrugged. "Everyone knows that your little playmates are always sophisticated women of the world. I'm sure a 'Juliet type' like me would bore you to tears in no time," she said sarcastically.

Donovan smiled sensually, and, reaching out, ran his hand caressingly along the curve of her cheek. She gasped at the sensation that brought her body to tingling life. A gleam of triumph lit his eyes, as though her reaction gave him a tigerish pleasure.

"Perhaps I'm bored with my usual women," he suggested silkily. "It was you who said Juliet was a sexy lady. Perhaps I would find it interesting to explore that premise more thoroughly."

She stepped back hurriedly, and he let her go, his hand leaving her face reluctantly. Even when he was no longer touching her she could still feel the tug of his overpowering virility. She was tempted to move closer to him, so that she might again feel that tingling aliveness she had never known before.

She forced her voice to coolness. "I don't find that very likely. I think you came here tonight to soothe Charles' feelings for rejecting his protégée, but when you saw me again, you couldn't resist the opportunity to try to get a little of your own back for the insults I tossed at you this afternoon."

There was a flicker of anger behind the blue eyes, and his mouth tightened fractionally. "So young to be so cynical," he said dryly. "Is it only me, or do you hate all men?"

"I don't hate men," Brenna said quietly. "I just don't find them fair or trustworthy where women are concerned."

"Interesting," Donovan said briefly, his eyes keen. She had the odd impression that those calculating eyes had observed, analyzed, and stored up for future use every facet of her physical and mental faculties.

"In this case, you're wrong," he said casually, reaching into a back pocket to draw out a folded, wrinkled manuscript. He held it out to her. "I came to give you this."

She took the script curiously. Printed in large letters on the title page was *Forgotten Moment.* She looked up, startled.

"I want you for the role of Mary Durney," Donovan said quietly. "Charles said you were a quick study."

Brenna nodded dazedly, looking down at the script.

"You'll have to be," Donovan said grimly. "I want you ready for filming in three days."

She looked at him. "I don't understand," she said in confusion. "The trade papers said production started on *Forgotten Moment* two months ago. Mary Durney was being played by some Broadway actress."

"She's not working out. I'm replacing

45

her," Donovan said.

Brenna shivered at the ruthlessness in his voice. "Just like that?" she asked faintly.

"Just like that," he said implacably. He went on, "Mary Durney is a supporting role, but I think you'll find her worthwhile. Played right, she could steal the film."

"Why me?" Brenna asked bluntly.

"Because you're right for her," Donovan said simply. "When Charles asked me to audition you for Angie, he said you had a quality that grabbed a person by the throat and didn't let go."

"You make me sound like a boa constrictor," Brenna said wryly.

"I have a hunch you can be just as lethal to a man," he said lightly, before his tone became coolly businesslike again. "He was right: You have a quality I want. But not for Angie. For Mary Durney."

"For such a devoted mother, you're being shockingly neglectful, Brenna," Blake Conroy said nastily. She had been so involved with Michael Donovan's astounding proposal that she hadn't noticed Conroy's approach. Conroy sauntered over to her, holding a tousled and drowsy Randy, who looked as if he had been snatched up from a deep sleep. He probably had, Brenna thought furiously. She brought Randy to almost all the rehearsals. He played or slept in his playpen in the wings. The cast had adopted him; Conroy was the one person who never had time for Randy. He was obviously hoping to use the baby now in some ploy to get back at her for her rejection this evening. She snatched Randy from him, cuddling the warm, sturdy body protectively.

Conroy surveyed her with sly satisfaction before turning to Donovan, who had gone strangely still. "Touching isn't it?" he drawled caustically. "I thought you'd better realize what you're letting yourself in for before committing yourself. It's a package deal with Brenna, you know. She's quite boringly obsessed with that kid of hers." With a mocking salute, he strolled away, eminently well satisfied with himself.

Michael Donovan's face was expressionless as he asked slowly, "The child is yours?"

"My name's on his birth certificate," Brenna said flippantly. She felt strangely vulnerable before those penetrating eyes. She hugged Randy closer, until he gave a sleepy little grunt.

"And who else's name is on that birth certificate, Brenna?" Donovan asked softly, his blue eyes gleaming fiercely. "Who is the father?"

She could see that, for some reason, he was in a white hot rage. She wondered briefly if he objected to his actresses having family commitments.

"There's no other name on Randy's birth certificate," she said coolly. "It's not required when the child's parents aren't married."

"How old is he?" Donovan asked hoarsely.

"Two," Brenna answered.

"My God, you started young, didn't you?" he asked bitterly. "You must have been barely eighteen when you gave birth to him."

Brenna lifted her head defiantly. "Perhaps you should have given me the role of Angie after all," she said sweetly. "You can see we have a lot in common."

"Yes, I can see that," Donovan said tightly, the flame in the electric blue eyes scorching her.

"Perhaps you would like to retract your offer," Brenna said scornfully. "It might not be very good publicity to have an unwed mother in your precious picture."

"To hell with the publicity," Donovan said roughly. "No one tells me who to cast in my pictures. You're going to be Mary Durney, Brenna."

His arrogant declaration only aggravated

the antagonism that his very presence generated in her.

"If I choose to be," she said firmly.

His mocking glance ran over her faded jeans and simple white tailored shirt.

"Oh, you'll choose to be," he said coolly. "I gather your lover isn't offering you and the baby support. You'd be a fool to turn down financial security for you and your child."

Brenna's face flushed at this humiliating reference to her obvious poverty. "Money isn't everything, Mr. Donovan," she said tersely. "Randy is a very happy, contented child. We don't need your money."

"Don't you, Brenna?" he asked lazily. "Think about it. My private number is on the script. Read it tonight, and let me know." He turned to go, and then wheeled back, his gaze sharp as a surgeon's scalpel. "One thing, Brenna," he said tautly. "If your baby's father is still hanging around, get rid of him. Once you're working for me, I don't want him near you!"

He walked quickly away, leaving her to stare after him, her lips parted in amazement.

THREE

Three hours later Brenna threw the script down in frustration, realizing that Donovan was right again. She must play this role, no matter how she felt about the arrogant Michael Donovan.

Why couldn't Mary Durney have been a sickly sweet character or a self-pitying martyr, so that she could have tossed the role back into Donovan's face, Brenna wondered gloomily. Mary Durney was innocent but no prim miss. She had humor, strength, and warmth. Brenna was convinced that she could make Mary Durney live, and she desperately wanted the chance to do just that. Damn Michael Donovan!

She reached for the phone on the table, and flipped the script back to the title page on which Donovan had scrawled his number in bold black numerals. Not allowing herself to think, she rapidly dialed the number. What if it was almost two in the morning?

she thought maliciously. He had told her to call him when she had read it, hadn't he? The idea of rousing Donovan from a sound sleep gave her a degree of satisfaction that surprised her. She had never been a spiteful girl. What was it about this man that made her want to strike out at him in any way she could?

The phone was answered on the second ring, and Donovan sounded disappointingly wide awake. When she had identified herself, he said impatiently, "I didn't expect it to be anyone else, Brenna."

"Well." She drew a deep breath. "I want to do it," she said rapidly.

There was a long silence on the other end and then a low chuckle. "I assume you mean the part," he drawled mockingly.

Color flooded her face at the innuendo, and she silently cursed both her inept tongue and the taunting redheaded devil on the other end of the line.

"You know I mean the part," she said angrily.

"Yes, unfortunately I do," he said lightly. She could almost see the amused grin on his face. Then his voice became cool and businesslike. "I trust you can be ready to leave by two this afternoon. You can fly up with me in the Lear jet. We're filming at

Twin Pines, you know."

She hadn't known. It hadn't occurred to her that she would have to leave Los Angeles. It should have, of course. Nearly all of Donovan's pictures were shot at Twin Pines now, when not on location. Her mind moved frantically. She'd have to notify the clerical agency, and Randy's nursery school, and Vivian, of course. She knew Charles would be glad to replace her in the play.

"I can leave today," she said slowly. "But you needn't bother yourself about arrangements. I prefer to drive."

"Don't be ridiculous," Donovan said impatiently. "I want you there this evening."

"Then I'll start early," she said stubbornly. There was no way she was going to see more of Michael Donovan than was absolutely necessary. He had a most unsettling effect on her. "Traveling with a baby can be very cumbersome, Mr. Donovan. I prefer to travel by car."

"You're taking the child?" he asked, his tone flat.

"Of course," Brenna said coolly. "Do you have any objections?"

"None at all," he said absently. "I should have expected it, I suppose. I'll work something out."

Brenna wondered what he had to work

out. "Then I'll see you this evening," she said firmly. "Good night, Mr. Donovan." She replaced the phone without giving him a chance to object, and leaned back against the cushions of the couch, her head in a whirl. She wondered dazedly how she was going to get everything done, and still leave in the early morning to keep her promise to be at Twin Pines by early evening.

Well, first things first. She must get a few hours' sleep if she was to drive all day. She turned out the light and walked briskly into the bedroom. She set the alarm for six, shrugged out of her navy robe, and settled down to try to sleep.

The alarm came too soon. Brenna felt as tired as when she went to sleep. She took a cold shower, standing under the spray until she at least felt alive again. She brushed her hair and dressed hurriedly in rust-colored high waisted pants and a buttercup-yellow shirt that made her hair gleam in a glossy contrast. No time for makeup, she decided. She made herself a cup of instant coffee, added milk and sugar and carried it to the bedroom to sip as she packed. There was more to pack for Randy than for herself. Her own wardrobe was meager to say the least, but a two-year-old had to have a minimun of at least three changes a day. In the middle of her packing Randy awoke and she had to stop and dress him. After depositing him in his playpen in the living room, she hurried back to resume her packing, ignoring his loud protests. Randy always got up in the morning with a voracious appetite and wanted to eat first thing. She knew she couldn't put off his breakfast for very long, but she wanted to finish packing this suitcase before she stopped again. She had just put the last items in and closed the lid, when the doorbell rang. Who in the world could be at the door at seven in the morning, she wondered.

"Just a minute," she called frantically, trying to fasten the bulging suitcase. She succeeded, only to have it spring open again. "Damn!" she muttered impatiently, giving up temporarily.

On her way to the door, she stopped to pick up a teddy bear that Randy had tossed out of the playpen, and gave it back to that howling individual resignedly. "I know, love," she said with a quick kiss on his silky head. Her sympathy was met by another bellow. She restrained herself forcibly from picking up the mournful little figure and comforting him. She'd never get out of here if she gave in to Randy's pleadings.

The doorbell rang again, and she tore herself from Randy's clinging arms with some difficulty. Randy renewed his heartbroken wailing, and she ran her fingers through her hair in exasperation.

She marched to the door and threw it open, her brow creased in a frown. "What is it?" she asked crossly of the man in jeans and sweatshirt, who stood appraising her coolly.

"You shouldn't open your door without first checking to see who's on the other side, you know," the man said disapprovingly. "I'm Monty Walters. Michael Donovan sent me."

She should have known, Brenna thought with irritation, glaring balefully at the man standing before her. Did Donovan infect all the people around him with his own arrogant bossiness?

"May I come in?" Walters asked politely, stepping forward so that she was forced to give way or be trampled underfoot. A little over middle height, he was in his late twenties, with crisp dark curly hair that framed a face that was surprisingly boyish. The dark eyes, however, were completely adult and just a little cynical.

After the night and morning she had gone through, Brenna was not about to be intimidated by one of Donovan's underlings.

"I'm sorry, Mr. Walters, but I haven't the time to talk to you right now," she said shortly. "Any last minute instructions Mr. Donovan has for me will have to wait until I arrive at Twin Pines."

There was a flicker of surprise in the dark eyes, and Walters looked at her with new interest. "That's why I'm here," he said coolly. "Mr. Donovan didn't care for the idea of your driving yourself. I'm to personally escort you and the child to the complex."

"That won't be necessary. I can drive myself perfectly well," Brenna said between her teeth.

Walters closed the door behind him firmly. "It may not be necessary for you, Miss Sloan," he said dryly. "But it's of the utmost necessity to me, if I want to keep my job." He looked around appraisingly. "Now I suggest that we get moving. If you'll supply me with the names and telephone numbers of people you want to advise of your departure, I'll attend to that, while you look after your child." He flinched as Randy emitted another piercing howl.

"He's hungry," Brenna said defensively, as she moved toward the playpen.

"Then I suggest you feed him," Monty

Walters said bluntly. "But first give me those phone numbers."

Without knowing quite why she was giving in to this aggressive young man, Brenna found herself meekly supplying him with the necessary information. Then she picked up Randy and headed for the tiny kitchenette, where she prepared his usual oatmeal, bacon, and orange juice. Once fed, he regained his sunny disposition, and permitted her to put him back in his playpen with a toy. She swiftly washed and dried the dishes and tidied up the kitchen, then went back to the bedroom to resume her packing.

When she came out of the bedroom, Walters had already disassembled the portable playpen and high chair and set them neatly by the door, and Randy was sitting on the couch playing with a chain of fascinating colored keys. Monty Walters was standing before the window, his eyes narrowed appraisingly.

"Stained glass," he said, admiring the rich violet and blue of the floral design. "Quite lovely and unexpected. Your work?"

Brenna nodded, thawing a bit at his admiration. She was very proud of that window. "It seemed appropriate," she said, making a face. "You've probably noticed this neighborhood is not high on aesthetic views."

"So you made your own," he observed, looking around the room with new interest. Cream walls provided a classic frame for the window. The furniture was in neutral shades and far from new, and the glowing beauty of the hardwood floor was accented by several brightly colored throw rugs.

"You've done a lot with it," he said thoughtfully, his eyes returning to the window, which was the focal point of the room. "An unusual hobby," he commented.

"It's becoming increasingly popular," she said quietly. "I learned it at school." The children's home had been convinced that idle hands bred mischief and the children had been offered arts and crafts classes of all descriptions.

"I've always thought a person's home reflected a great deal of their personality," Walters said quietly, turning his gaze to regard Brenna soberly. "I like your home, Miss Sloan. I have a hunch you're not just another pretty face."

"If that's a compliment, I thank you, kind sir," she said lightly. "I'm sure you're not just a pretty face, either."

He smiled ruefully. "Did I sound chauvinistic?" he said, shaking his head. "I haven't made a very good impression on you, have I? I guess my pride was a bit hurt at being used as a glorified chauffeur, and I took it out on you." His smile widened appealingly. "Shall we start over?"

Brenna answered his smile with a warm one of her own. "I think we'd better. It's a long way to the Oregon border." She made a face. "No one would have voted me Miss Congeniality this morning either."

"You're right there," he said impudently, dark eyes twinkling. "Now shall we hit the road, before I manage to alienate you completely?"

Together they packed the Lincoln Continental to its spacious limits. When Brenna had objected to leaving her own car in Los Angeles, Monty had countered that the trip would be much more comfortable in the Lincoln, and Donovan had already arranged for her car to be picked up in a few days. There could be no argument about the drive being more comfortable, she admitted to herself, when they were on their way. The car was the height of luxury. She stroked the wine velvet upholstery of the seat with almost sensual pleasure.

"It's a lovely car," she commented. "Does it belong to Mr. Donovan?"

Monty Walters shook his head with a grin,

as he maneuvered the big silver car onto the freeway. "It's mine," he admitted. "I have a vulgar passion for ostentatious cars, but I haven't dared to indulge it until recently."

"Money?" Brenna asked. This car must have cost a small fortune. Though Michael Donovan was reputed to pay his employees very well, she found it unlikely that even the most generous salary would provide a luxury of this magnitude.

"In a manner of speaking." He gave her a sheepish grin. "You see I'm stinking rich."

Her mouth quirked at the boyish awkwardness of this revelation. "I'm afraid I don't see your problem," she said solemnly. "Why couldn't you have a car like this, if you could afford it?"

"I didn't want to remind Donovan that I was wealthy, so I've been driving a '75 Volkswagon for the past two years," he said simply. "It's only lately that I've felt confident enough to risk the Lincoln."

Brenna stared at him in amazement. "Do you mean Michael Donovan would have objected to you buying the car of your choice with your own money?" she asked indignantly. That an aggressive, confident man like Monty could be so intimidated was truly incredible.

"Hell, no!" he said explosively. "But after

working like the devil to get this job, I thought I'd better play it low key. He knew my background when he hired me and he was dubious, to say the least, about my willingness to stick to the kind of work schedule he demanded of his employees." His mouth twisted wryly. "I soon understood why. Simon Legree has nothing on Michael Donovan."

"Yet, you're still with him," Brenna observed.

"I guess I'm just a masochist," Walters said lightly. Reaching out he touched a button, and taped music flooded the car with the mellow strains of a Barry Manilow hit. Brenna leaned back and relaxed on the plush velvet seats, letting the strain of the last few hours flow out of her.

In the next several hours Brenna found Monty Walters to be amazingly companionable. He was quick-witted and energetic, with a wry sense of humor that was almost puckish. By the time they had shared lunch, dinner, and almost eight hours of desultory conversation, she felt as if they were old friends.

It was nearing twilight when they crossed the Oregon border, and a brief twenty minutes later they reached Twin Pines.

She didn't know what she had expected of

Donovan's Twin Pines complex. Perhaps in the back of her mind had been the idea that it would be the usual movie studio lot like Paramount or Universal. She should have known better.

Twin Pines was as unique as the man who had created it. Located at the edge of a small Oregon lumber town, it looked more like a country club than a movie studio, with low modernistic buildings in redwood and glass, wide streets, and several tree-shaded park areas furnished with picnic tables and benches.

"Impressed?" Walters asked, arching his eyebrows quizzically, as she turned back to him from her eager perusal of the passing scene.

"Who wouldn't be?" she asked dryly. "It's perfectly charming, but not exactly what you'd expect of Michael Donovan."

"On the contrary, it's exactly what you'd expect of him," Walters said briskly. "He's gathered the most gifted and skilled people in the industry here at Twin Pines. People that usually work freelance have been formed into a sort of repertory group. When they're working, he drives them unmercifully. It's just good sense to provide them with the most pleasant surroundings possible to enjoy in their free time."

"You admire him very much, don't you?" Brenna asked curiously.

"You're damn right I do," he replied unequivocally. "There are a few men in every generation who combine creative genius with irresistible drive. When you find one, if you're smart, you grab hold of his coattails and let him carry you to the top."

"I wouldn't have thought you'd be interested in a free ride," Brenna said thoughtfully.

Walters snorted derisively. "There's nothing free about it. Donovan extracts the last ounce of effort from the people around him. You give until you have nothing else to give. Then, somehow, you find he has expanded your limits, so that there is a whole new reservoir for him to tap." His dark eyes were reflective. "He's a complete workaholic, a nit-picking perfectionist, and a totally ruthless exploiter of the talents of his employees," he continued, almost beneath his breath. "But, by God, it's worth it!"

"You don't paint a very comforting picture of my new boss," Brenna said wryly.

"I didn't mean to," Walters said bluntly. "If you need a security blanket, you have no business around Donovan. He'll tear you to pieces."

"I can believe that," she said with a shrug,

remembering Donovan's steamroller tactics in her own case. "Well, I can always leave if I find him too impossible," she said lightly.

He shot her an appraising glance. "I wouldn't count on that," he said coolly. "I have an idea that Donovan has plans for you. And Donovan always gets what he wants."

"Plans?" Brenna asked blankly. She shook her head. "I have a small supporting role in one of his pictures. I'm not important in his scheme of things. What plans could he possibly have for me?"

"Who knows?" Monty said, with a shrug. "Maybe he sees you as the next Sarah Bernhardt." He grinned boyishly. "Whatever it is, you're being given very special treatment, Brenna Sloan. I'll have you know, I'm a very important cog in Donovan's organization," he said with mock conceit. "It's not an ordinary occurrence for me to be ordered to act as chauffeur to an unknown actress. I must admit that my ego was very badly dented when he gave me my instructions."

She smiled in amusement. "I hate to disillusion you, but I'm afraid your original supposition was correct."

He slanted her an oblique smile. "We'll see," he said composedly.

He pulled into a circular driveway that led

64

to a long two-story building, which, like the other buildings in the complex, was constructed of redwood, stone, and glass.

"Employee's quarters," Monty said briskly, in answer to her inquiring look. "You'll find your accommodations are part of your fringe benefits. You're provided with a small apartment at Donovan's expense. The units also supply maid service at your own expense. There's a cafeteria in each residence hall that is open twenty-four hours a day." He grimaced. "They have to be. There are times when we work around the clock to meet the demands of our lord and master."

He pulled to a smooth stop before the front entrance, jumped out, and came around the car with the characteristic energy she was beginning to associate with him.

A husky, sandy-haired teenager in a plaid shirt and jeans came hurrying out the front entrance, and opened the passenger door quickly.

"Good to see you back, Mr. Walters," he said respectfully.

"Thanks, Johnny," Walters said easily, as he helped Brenna from the car.

"This is Johnny Smith, Brenna. He's a sort of jack-of-all-trades. If you need something, ask Johnny."

Brenna smiled warmly at the boy and he smiled back. "You bet," he said cheerfully. "I'll take good care of you, miss."

"Thank you, Johnny," she said quietly.

Monty Walters opened the rear door, and lifted a sleeping Randy out with the utmost care to avoid waking him. He tossed the trunk keys to the boy. "Bring in Miss Sloan's luggage, will you, Johnny?"

Walters escorted her into the bright, cheerful lobby, and paused before the reception desk. A pert, dark-haired girl looked up with a smile that took on a flattering obsequiousness as soon as she recognized Walters.

"Paula Drummond, Brenna," Walters said briskly. "This is Brenna Sloan, Paula. I understand Mr. Donovan's secretary was to contact you with regard to the arrangements."

The dark-haired girl shook her head. "Mr. Donovan called himself," she said solemnly. "It's a pleasure to meet you, Miss Sloan. We have everything arranged just as Mr. Donovan instructed." She picked up the phone and punched several buttons rapidly. "Doris, Miss Sloan is here. Would you come down right away?" She turned to Brenna and Walters, a bright smile on her face.

"We've given you one of the guest cottages. I hope you'll be very comfortable there. If there's anything else you need, just call me."

"Thank you. I'm sure everything will be fine," Brenna said awkwardly, a little uneasy over the effusiveness of the receptionist.

"A guest cottage?" Monty asked thoughtfully, with a low whistle. "That's really royal treatment, Brenna. Cottages are reserved for stars and visiting VIPs."

"Then there must be a mistake," Brenna said firmly. "We both know that I'm neither."

"There's no mistake, Miss Sloan," Paula Drummond spoke up quickly. "Mr. Donovan's instructions were very explicit." She looked beyond Brenna to smile at the young woman who had just gotten off the elevator and was crossing the lobby toward them. "This is Doris Charles, Miss Sloan."

Doris Charles was a woman in her middle twenties with short curly red hair and rather plain features that were illuminated by a warm smile. She held out a strong square hand and shook Brenna's hand vigorously. "I'm very happy to meet you, Miss Sloan." She turned immediately toward Walters, who was still holding Randy, and said briskly. "I'll take him." She held out her arms, and Walters obediently put the child into them. Brenna stared in bewilderment as the red-haired woman cuddled the child expertly, her face softening as she looked down at him. "What a little darling he is," she said softly. "His name's Randy, I believe?"

"That's right," Brenna said, confused. "But who are you?"

Doris Charles looked up at her, a small frown creasing her forehead. "I'm your son's nurse. Mr. Donovan flew me up from Los Angeles to care for Randy." she said calmly. "I believe you'll find I have the highest qualifications."

"I'm sure you have," Brenna said tiredly, her head whirling. "But I don't need a nurse, Miss Charles. I take care of Randy myself."

Johnny Smith came into the lobby laden with suitcases that he put down in front of the desk.

"Don't be too hasty, Brenna," Walters said easily. "You'll need someone to care for Randy while you're working. Miss Charles is well qualified to do just that."

Brenna nodded slowly at the logic of Monty's reasoning. "You're right, Monty," she admitted, and smiled at Doris Charles. The red-haired woman seemed to be loving as well as efficient. "I'll be glad to have your help with Randy, Miss Charles," she said warmly.

"Doris," the nurse said briefly, grinning back at her. "I'll take the greatest care of your son, Miss Sloan," she promised.

Paula Drummond cleared her throat gently, and said tentatively. "Now, if you'll tell me which of these bags are your personal possessions, Miss Sloan, I'll have Johnny take them to the cottage. He can come back and take the baby's things to Miss Charles' apartment later."

"What are you talking about?" Brenna asked blankly. "Everything goes to the cottage. Randy is staying with me."

Paula Drummond shook her head. "No, ma'am," she said, "Mr. Donovan was quite definite on that point. Only you are to occupy the cottage. The baby is to remain at the residence hall with Miss Charles."

"I don't care how definite Mr. Donovan was on the subject," Brenna said between her teeth. "I am not being separated from my baby." The nerve of the man, she fumed. Casually disposing of her child like an unwanted parcel. "I don't care where you put me," she went on grimly. "I don't need any fancy cottage, anywhere will do. But wherever it is, I want my child with me."

There was a shocked look on the receptionist's face. "But you don't understand, Miss Sloan," she stammered. "I can't go against Mr. Donovan's orders."

"I'm not going anywhere without Randy," Brenna said flatly. "So you are going to have to, aren't you?"

"It's just not possible," Paula Drummond said, almost in tears. "Please be reasonable, Miss Sloan. Mr. Donovan will be most displeased."

Brenna had opened her mouth to tell the girl what Michael Donovan could do with his displeasure, when Walters interjected smoothly. "You can't do anything about it tonight, Brenna. Paula is only obeying orders, and you'll only get her in trouble. Why don't you go along with the arrangements right now. When you see Mr. Donovan, you can speak to him about making any necessary changes."

The voice of reason again, Brenna thought impatiently, wishing she could fault the argument. She was beginning to understand why Monty had risen so quickly at Donovan Enterprises Ltd. He was a very persuasive gentleman.

"Okay. I'll do as you suggest for the present," Brenna said reluctantly. "But I want to speak to Mr. Donovan right away, Monty."

Monty Walters nodded, ignoring Paula Drummond's outraged gasp. He understood the receptionist's incredulity. One didn't demand an audience with Michael Donovan in his own kingdom of Twin Pines. Such an act was unprecedented, but then so were all Donovan's actions in regard to Brenna Sloan. Perhaps Donovan's reception of her request would be in accordance with this exceptional behavior.

"Mr. Donovan asked me to call him when we arrived," he said quietly. "I'll ask him to get in touch with you." He touched Brenna's cheek lightly. "It's been a long day. Why don't you try to take a nap? You look exhausted."

Brenna nodded ruefully. She probably looked a wreck. With only four hours' sleep last night and the long drive today, she felt achingly tired. "I will," she promised, smiling. "Thank you for everything, Monty."

"My pleasure, Brenna," he said lightly. "I'll see you soon, no doubt." With a casual wave, he turned and walked out the door.

"Well, now that we're all in agreement, we'll get you settled, Miss Sloan," Paula Drummond said brightly. "Which are your bags?"

As she silently pointed out her personal luggage, Brenna was tempted to tell the girl

71

that they were not all in agreement. There was no way that Michael Donovan was going to get away with this high-handed interference in her personal life. As she gave Doris Charles a few quiet instructions as to Randy's likes and dislikes as to food and his general schedule, she already felt a sense of loss. She and Randy had never spent even one night apart, and she was feeling distinctly shaky at the idea of the parting. He had become the center of her life since Janine died.

"I'll take good care of him," Doris Charles said kindly. "It's only a five-minute walk to the cottage. You can come and see him as often as you wish."

Brenna felt an absurd desire to say thank you. Thank you for telling me I can come and see my own child. She already felt he had been taken away from her. "I know you will," she said huskily, "and it's only for tonight." She brushed the top of Randy's head with a light kiss, and turned away quickly before she changed her mind. She followed Johnny Smith out the far door and down the paved path toward the small, elegant redwood cottage.

Four

Johnny Smith unlocked the front door and touched the wall switch, flooding the interior with light. He preceded her into the room, saying cheerfully, "I'll just carry these on through to the bedroom, Miss Sloan." Taking her silence as assent, he crossed the deeply carpeted living room to a door on the left, leaving Brenna to gaze in amazed admiration at the interior of the cottage.

The living room area was carpeted in pearl gray with matching drapes at the casement windows. The modern furniture was in shades of violet and purple with cream pillows thrown in luxurious profusion on the lavender couch. Clear glass occasional tables gave a tranquil, pristine quality to the living room. In the dining area, a silver bowl with a multitude of floating violets was the colorful centerpiece on a magnificent glass dining table. There appeared to be a small kitchenette leading off the dining area, but she decided not to explore further, and followed Johnny into the bedroom.

Brenna found that the boy had pulled open the drapes and was coming out of the adjoining bathroom. "Plenty of towels," he said briskly. "Sometimes the maids forget."

The bedroom, too, was carpeted in pearl gray with the same violet accents, she noticed. The queen-sized bed was covered with a royal purple taffeta spread, coordinating with the matching drapes at the long French windows.

Johnny pointed to the cream princess phone on the side table. "You dial nine to get an outside line, dial six to get the main hall switchboard." His bright, brown eyes were eager. "Would you like for me to bring you something from the cafeteria, Miss Sloan? It wouldn't be any trouble."

Brenna shook her head, smiling. "No, thank you, Johnny," she said. "Mr. Walters and I stopped for dinner earlier." She realized with a little shock of surprise that this teenager was only a little younger than herself, yet she felt a million years removed from his youthful enthusiasm.

Johnny nodded, and walked briskly to the front door. "The kitchen is well stocked if you feel like a bite later," he said, and then grinned engagingly. "I'm a great one for midnight snacks, myself."

"Me, too," Brenna confided solemnly, from where she stood in the bedroom doorway.

"Be sure and tell the desk if you need me," he said, and with a final grin he quietly closed the door.

Brenna stood there for a moment, feeling a great sense of aloneness sweep over her as the door shut on that cheerful presence. Looking around the exquisite apartment, she wondered dazedly what she was doing in all this luxury. She didn't belong here. She belonged in that small apartment in Los Angeles with Randy. Then she squared her shoulders determinedly. She was just tired and dispirited over the separation from Randy. This was a great opportunity. She would be an idiot to let herself become intimidated by these rich surroundings. She was the same Brenna Sloan here as in her own apartment in Los Angeles. All she had to do was to hold to that truth with both hands, and she'd be all right.

She considered making herself a cup of hot chocolate, but decided not to bother. She was suddenly unutterably weary. Opening a suitcase, she pulled out a white jersey tailored robe and shower cap, and drifted into the bathroom. She noticed, without surprise, the lavender tub and gray and crystal accessories.

She made the shower a brief but thorough one, wanting only to sample the softness of the queen-sized bed. After toweling off on the huge fluffy towel on the heated rack, she slipped on her robe and gave her hair a lick and a promise with the brush she found on the built-in glass vanity. Then with a sigh of contentment she lay down on the bed, not even bothering to remove the spread. She'd get up and unpack soon, she thought drowsily as her lids closed. And she wanted to be sure to talk to Donovan about Randy tonight. She tried to force her weighted lids open again, knowing she should try to call Donovan before she gave in to this delicious sleepiness. That was the last thought that surfaced before she fell soundly asleep.

It seemed only a moment before she was awakened by a thundering cacophony of sound. She moaned and rolled over, trying to ignore it, but it continued interminably until she realized it was someone at the front door. She sat up, and slowly rose to her feet. Catching sight of the clock on the bedside table, she realized groggily that it was almost ten. She had slept for almost two hours! It wasn't enough she realized, as she stumbled bleary-eyed out of the bedroom, across the living room to the front door, and fumbled with the lock.

She wasn't even surprised to see an extremely angry Michael Donovan on the doorstep. Leaning her head against the door, she peered at him owlishly, observing that he looked as vital and alive as ever in figure-hugging black cords and a black turtleneck sweater, his hair a dark flame above the sombre garments. She wondered sleepily if there was such a thing as an energy vampire. Just the sight of his electric-charged vitality made her feel tired — more tired, she corrected herself drowsily.

"Hello, Mr. Donovan," she said, yawning.

"Good evening, Miss Sloan," he said sarcastically. "I hope I didn't disturb you." He pushed the door open, and brushed by her, closing the door behind him with a resounding slam. She flinched at the sound, as well as at the obvious untruth. It was quite evident that Donovan was not at all sorry to have awakened her. He strode into the center of the living room, and turned to regard her impatiently, looking outrageously out of place in the delicate grays and violets of the room. Like a pirate at a royal garden party, she thought dimly.

"I understand you wanted to see me," he said sarcastically. "I tried to phone you, and it rang off the hook, so I came over."

"You phoned me?" she asked sleepily, trailing behind him into the living room. "You must have called the wrong number," she said tiredly, gravitating toward the lavender couch, and curling up in the corner. "I would have heard it."

"I did *not* call a wrong number," he said between clenched teeth. He moved with pantherish grace to the gray extension phone on the glass end table, and checked the phone quickly. "You have the volume turned off," he said disgustedly, adjusting the dial. "It's hardly courteous to ask me to get in touch with you, and then turn the telephone off, Miss Sloan," he said curtly, his blue eyes blazing.

She felt the stirrings of indignation at the unfair accusation, but she was still too sluggish to take umbrage. "I didn't turn down the volume," she said lifelessly. "It must have been the previous occupant of the cottage."

Donovan's eyes narrowed as they raked over her. "What the hell is the matter with you?" he demanded roughly. "Are you on something?"

"On something?" she asked vaguely. Then realizing what he meant, she woke up with a vengeance. She sat up straight on the couch, swift color pinking her cheeks.

"I do not take drugs, Mr. Donovan!" she said angrily. "I'm merely very sleepy."

He shrugged. "It's an understandable assumption. Your generation seems partial to crutches."

"And yours wasn't?" she inquired sarcastically. "I believe yours was known as the protest generation. You started the whole drug culture."

"Touché," he said ruefully. "Not me personally, I assure you." His gaze ran over her lingeringly. "Are you always so slow to wake up?" he asked abruptly.

"Not everyone wakes up all in one piece," she said resentfully. "Though I'm sure you're one of those who switch on like an electric light."

"Yes, I am," he said absently, his eyes thoughtful. "One of us will have to change," he said obscurely.

She stared at him in confusion, but before she could voice a question he continued curtly. "Monty said there was some problem with your living arrangements. What is so important that it couldn't wait until tomorrow?" he demanded, looking around the richly furnished room casually. "Everything seems to be in order."

"Everything is not in order!" she said

hotly, rising to her feet and facing him belligerently. "Randy isn't here with me."

The keen blue eyes became suddenly watchful. "The child?" he asked carefully. "I made adequate provisions for him. Doris Charles has excellent references, and her apartment has been furnished with everything a child could possibly want."

"Everything but his mother," Brenna grated, her hands clenching into fists. "I want him with me!"

Donovan strolled over to the small portable bar in the corner, and poured himself a Scotch and water, before turning to face her.

"That won't be possible," he said coolly. "I prefer that the child be cared for in the residence hall. You'll need all your concentration for the next week or so. I don't want you distracted by maternal worries."

"That's ridiculous," she said angrily. "I've always taken care of Randy myself, and I assure you that my schedule has been more demanding than you can imagine."

"But not as taxing as the one I'll ask of you," he said bluntly. "There are a number of scenes that have to be reshot, as well as the rest of the picture to finish, and I fully intend to bring the picture in on schedule, Brenna," he said forcefully.

"I've agreed to accept Miss Charles' assistance," Brenna said in exasperation. "What difference could it possibly make if she and Randy move in here?"

He took a long swallow of his drink before he answered. "It makes a difference to me. In case you haven't noticed, I run things here."

"So I've been told," she said bitterly, her brown eyes suddenly bright with unshed tears as she gazed pleadingly at him. "Why should you object to me having my son here?" she asked huskily. "Won't you change your mind?"

His eyes were brooding as he met hers across the room. "No, I won't change my mind," he said harshly. "I don't want him here, Brenna."

"But why?" she asked distractedly. "You can't just arbitrarily refuse without giving me a reason."

His eyes narrowed to steely slits, and she knew she had angered him. He carefully put his unfinished drink on the bar, and said coolly, "You want to know my reason, Brenna? Then you shall have it." He crossed the space between them in three swift strides. "You're pushing me, Brenna. I hoped to have more time," he said softly.

"What do you mean?" she faltered, breathless at his sudden proximity.

He shrugged, the black knit of his sweater straining over powerful shoulders. "You're not ready for this yet," he said calmly, "but I'm tired of playing games." He looked directly into her eyes, and said deliberately, "I don't want your child here, because it drives me crazy to see you with him."

Brenna couldn't understand this incredible statement, and she looked up at him in total bewilderment. His two hands reached up to cup her face. "You see, I've discovered you were abysmally wrong about the type of woman that turns me on," he said huskily. "I want you, Brenna."

She felt as if she were being hypnotized by those piercing eyes that held her in a magnetic thrall. He was so close that she could feel the vibrant warmth emanating from him, the smell, the clean scent of soap and the indescribable essence of the male animal. "No," she cried, her eyes clinging to his. "It's crazy!"

"Do you think I don't know that?" he asked savagely. "Do you think I go around seducing twenty-year-old girls as a matter of course? I don't like this one iota." He drew a ragged breath, and spoke more calmly. "All that I know is that when I saw you at the audition yesterday afternoon, it was as if someone had punched me in the stomach. I wanted you more than I have ever wanted any woman in my life. I've got to have you, or go totally insane."

"You're already insane," she whispered. "Things just don't happen like that."

"I didn't think so either," he said harshly. "I seemed to have become completely obsessed by you. I never cared a damn about chastity in a woman before, but the thought of another man having had you before me, makes me want to strangle you."

His eyes gleamed with such savagery that a flicker of fear shot through her, and she took an involuntary step backward. His hands fell away from her, and his mouth twisted cynically. "Don't worry, I haven't reached that stage of barbarism yet," he said hoarsely. "Though I just may, if I ever catch you with any other man. I can't even bear to see you with the child, knowing that another man fathered him."

"Why are you telling me all this?" she said dazedly. "First, you tell me you want some sort of affair with me, and then that you can't bear to have me around my own son." Her voice rose hysterically. "What am I supposed to do? Drown him? You're completely mad!"

He shrugged. "I knew it was too soon," he

said. "I was going to wait a little longer, until you got to know me better. I know it's a shock to you." His mouth twisted wryly. "As for the child, I'll just have to learn to tolerate him, won't I?"

"Tolerate?" The word added fuel to her growing anger. That anyone would have to "tolerate" the adorable, sunny imp that was Randy was unbelievable.

"I shouldn't bother," she said coldly. "Neither of us need your tolerance, Mr. Donovan."

"The outraged lioness in defense of her cub," he murmured mockingly. "Tell me, now that I've invited you into my bed, don't you think that we're on personal enough terms for you to call me Michael?"

"As our acquaintance will be ending right here and now, I hardly think it necessary," she said coolly, turning toward the bedroom door.

His hand caught her arm as she walked past him, and he whirled her around to face him. "You're not walking out, Brenna," he said grimly. "You've got a job to do."

"As your mistress?" she asked sarcastically, lifting her chin.

"Eventually," Donovan said coolly. "But at present I have a film to make, and you agreed to take the role of Mary Durney."

"Impossible," she said shortly. "I couldn't do it now."

"You'll do it," he said grimly. "The two things have nothing to do with each other. If you think I gave you the role to apply some sort of sexual harassment, you're wrong. I'll get you into my bed because you want to occupy it, and not for any other reason."

"Then you're going to be very disappointed," she said defiantly. "I'll never want you or any other man like that, Michael Donovan."

"I think you will," he said with narrowed eyes. "I have no small amount of experience with women, and I'd judge you to be highly combustible material indeed, Brenna Sloan."

"Then you'd be wrong," she said hotly, her denial all the more adamant for the furtive memory of that momentary weakness in the wings of the Rialto.

He shook his head, his face mocking. "I don't think so. It's natural that you should be bitter and afraid of initiating any new relationships. You've obviously been hurt by your affair with Randy's father. Seventeen is an extremely sensitive age for something as traumatic as that to happen to a young girl. It's no wonder you've been rejecting other men since then."

"How did you know I've been rejecting men?" Brenna asked. Then her eyes widened incredulously. "My God, you've had me investigated!" she whispered.

"Nothing so dramatic," he scoffed lightly. "I sent a man around to ask a few questions of the right people, that's all. I knew after I spoke to you at the theater last night that you had some sort of grudge against men. It's my experience that a thorough knowledge of one's adversary is the only basis for success."

"And what did you learn about me?" she asked proudly. "Was it worth your employee's time?"

"Not much," he said laconically. "You grew up in a children's home. You have a secretarial job with Edwards Temporary Agency. You're a devoted mother, pay your bills promptly, and are distinctly cool to any amorous young men who try to approach you."

"Doesn't that discourage you?" she asked caustically.

"Not in the least," he said calmly. "It gives me a good deal of satisfaction to know that you haven't been involved with any other man since Randy's father let you down. I told you I was very possessive about you, and I know damn well I can melt that ice around you, Brenna."

"You wouldn't say you're the least bit egotistical?" she asked sardonically.

"I believe in myself," he said simply. "I wouldn't have gotten as far as I have in life, if I didn't." His sensual lips curved mischievously. "I also believe in chemistry, and we have an abundance of that, believe me."

"So you expect me to go on with the picture as if this interview had never happened?" she asked wonderingly.

"Why not?" he asked coolly. "Now that everything is out in the open, we go back to square one. You need the work and I need an actress. The fact that I also need you as a woman shouldn't concern you unduly. After all, before we had this conversation, I was prepared to wait until you said you wanted me. I still am. I won't promise not to do my damnedest to make you want me, but I'm not about to drag you, kicking and screaming, into the nearest cave."

"Do I have your promise on that?" Brenna asked skeptically.

Donovan's mouth tightened with anger, and his blue eyes flashed. "I'm not accustomed to having my word questioned." He drew a deep breath, and his tension eased fractionally. "What a suspicious little girl you are, Brenna," he said mockingly. "You have my promise that I won't pounce until the picture is finished. After that, if I haven't persuaded you to my way of thinking, all promises are null and void. I'll get you any way I can."

She shivered at the implacable ruthlessness in the lean face. "Can't you see it's no use?" she asked pleadingly.

"No, I can't," he said with determination. "And before I leave here tonight, I'm going to make you realize just what we could have together."

Her gaze flew to his, her brown eyes reflecting the panic of a startled doe. "No," she protested breathlessly, struggling to free herself from his restraining hands gripping her arms. "You promised!"

His hands tightened relentlessly, drawing her inexorably closer, quelling her frantic struggles with effortless strength. "Stop fighting me, Brenna!" He groaned huskily. "Don't you know I have to have something to keep me from going crazy in the next few weeks?" Then she was in his arms, pressed against his muscular body and experiencing the burning heat of his male hardness through the thin jersey of her robe. It was almost as if she were totally naked and completely vulnerable in his arms.

"Let me go," she gasped, twisting desperately to escape the tormenting closeness that was branding her as his possession.

It was as if he didn't hear her. His face held only a glazed absorption. He closed his eyes, drawing in his breath raggedly. "God, I want you!"

His mouth covered hers with such a savage need that she felt that she was being absorbed into him, as if she were becoming a mere extension of the desire that consumed him. His lips covered her face and throat with hot kisses before returning to ravish her parted lips with a dizzying penetration. She groaned helplessly at the sheer sensual pleasure his teasing tongue produced. His hands moved in an agony of frustration, feverishly caressing her back and bottom, cupping and exploring the silken skin through the flimsy material of the robe.

She was swept up in a cyclone of sensation, her body feeling as weak as melted butter as she leaned helplessly against him. He gave a triumphant chuckle as he raised his head to stare down at her with barbaric satisfaction, the electric blue eyes blazing. With deliberate slowness, his eyes holding hers almost hypnotically, his hands loosened the tie at her waist and parted the robe. He stared in glazed anticipation at her silken curves. Brenna could feel a tide of emotion electrify her body at the intensity of emotion on his face. He wasn't even touching her, yet she could feel her breasts firming, their rosy peaks hardening as if he were caressing them. "Damn, you're lovely," he said hoarsely. "You're mine, aren't you? Tell me you belong to me."

Then without waiting for a reply, he lowered his mouth to those teasing peaks that were entreating his caress. His tongue toyed tormentingly with each luscious mound until she was shaking with the erotic reaction that he was arousing in her. She remembered how earlier in the evening she had mentally compared him to a vampire. She realized now, with a swift rush of panic, how correct the simile had been. He was using his overpowering sensual magnetism to drain the resistance from her, leaving her a chattel to an aching need that she had never known could exist.

He raised his head and then slowly closed the robe, tying the belt deftly. He gazed broodingly at her flushed face and soft bruised mouth. Then he caught his breath sharply as he encountered wide brown eyes that were shining with helpless wonder.

"God, don't look at me like that, sweetheart," he groaned huskily, burying his face in her silky brown hair. He carefully with-held his taut body from her pliant curves. "I'm within an inch of picking you up and carrying you into that bedroom and raping you." His teeth nibbled at her ear, causing delicious shivers to run through her body. "And it would be rape, because as willing as I can make that gorgeous body of yours, your mind is still rejecting me."

He rubbed his lower body against hers sensuously. "I don't want only a one night stand with you, love. We're going to be together a long, long time. I want your body, your mind, and your soul. I'm going to own you, Brenna Sloan."

For one mad moment she accepted that arrogant assertion of dominance with blind submission, willing to yield everything to regain the throbbing pleasure he had made her feel. Then the independence of a lifetime asserted itself with a rush of scalding shame. My God, what was she doing, she thought with a sick feeling in the pit of her stomach. Where was her pride and self-respect that she could be vanquished so easily by this man's sexual expertise? Was she to be like her mother and Janine, used by men for their own gratification, and then tossed aside like a piece of refuse?

His grip had automatically loosened at the

signs of her surrender, and with one lithe twist she was free of him. She moved quickly to the other side of the room before turning to face him. Her face was pale and taut, and she hugged her arms close to her body as if to form a physical barrier between them.

"Is the demonstration over?" she asked defiantly, lifting her chin proudly. "If it is, I wish you'd leave."

There was disappointment and a reluctant admiration in Donovan's face as he watched her with narrowed eyes. "I almost had you, sweetheart," he said thoughtfully. "I wonder where I went wrong."

"Your mistake was forgetting that I am my own person," she said coolly. "Not some sort of slave for your amusement. You won't get another chance."

His smile was mocking, and his eyes flashed recklessly. "Bad move, darling," he said gently. "Haven't you heard I can't resist a challenge?" Then as she stiffened defensively, he shook his head. "Not tonight. I think I've made enough progress for one night, don't you?"

A scarlet flush dyed her cheeks at the memory of how easily Donovan had brushed aside her defenses as if they didn't exist, leaving her so humiliatingly subservient to his passion and her own.

"Don't worry, Brenna, my promise still stands," he said, shaking his head ruefully. "Though I imagine I'll be taking a hell of a lot of cold showers in the near future." He grimaced. "It wouldn't be at all a bad idea right now."

He strolled back to the bar and picked up his half empty glass and finished the drink in one swallow. When he turned back to her, his demeanor was coolly impersonal.

"Tomorrow morning you'll be free to go over your lines. I'll have Monty pick you up at noon to take you to Sound Stage B. You'll need to be fitted for costumes and meet the director, Jake Dominic."

She should have been relieved at his return to a businesslike attitude, but she was conscious of an illogical resentment that he could so easily turn off his emotions when she was still a mass of quivering butterflies inside. With no little effort she succeeded in masking her discomposure.

"I'll be ready," she said icily, then the last part of his sentence struck home. "Jake Dominic is directing?"

Donovan nodded, his mouth twisting cynically. "I'm surprised you didn't know," he said dryly. "I thought everyone in the business kept up with Jake's activities. In bed and out."

That was a patent understatement, Brenna thought wryly. The entire world displayed an interest in the antics of filmdom's bad boy. Jake Dominic was totally brilliant, and the most sought after director in Hollywood. His success had closely paralleled the meteoric rise of Michael Donovan, and the two men were known to be good friends. His personal life was as attention getting as his career image. Fabulously wealthy in his own right, film success and his satanic good looks proved irresistible to women. Even in an industry where morals were notoriously loose, Dominic's reputation was scandalous. Though Donovan's affairs were legion, he guarded his privacy closely. Dominic, on the other hand, had a reckless disregard for publicity, and was constantly in the gossip columns.

"Jake Dominic," she repeated musingly. She wondered idly if she had fallen from the frying pan into the fire. Surely one rake of Donovan's calibre was enough to contend with.

Donovan's eyes narrowed dangerously. "He interests you?" he asked silkily. "I'm afraid you'll have to forget any aspirations in that direction. I've already told Jake that you're off limits."

She flushed with indignation at the thought of Donovan discussing his strictly dishonorable intentions toward her with his equally dissolute cohort. How dare he stake her out as if she were some kind of property! There was no way that she would admit that her interest in Dominic was less anticipatory than wary.

"From what I understand, Mr. Dominic doesn't take kindly to restrictions of any kind," she said coolly. "So we'll just have to wait and see, won't we?"

Donovan's eyes flickered. "Don't make the mistake of trying to score off me through Jake," he warned tightly. "He might be my best friend, but I'm not about to share you with him."

Brenna shrugged insolently, and opened her mouth to tell him just what she thought of his arrogant statement, when there was a brisk knock on the door.

Donovan's eyes flew to her face. "Are you expecting someone?" he asked sharply.

"Who would I be expecting?" she asked caustically. "I'm the new girl in town, remember?"

With a muttered curse he strode swiftly to the door and threw it open. He surveyed the man who stood there with extreme displeasure.

"What the hell are you doing here, Jake?" he growled sourly. "I thought I had made myself clear."

The deep masculine voice of their visitor was mocking. "You always make yourself clear, Michael. I'm not here to poach on your preserves. I'm here purely on business."

Donovan moved aside reluctantly. "It better be damn pure," he said bluntly, as the other man strolled into the room. "You haven't had a platonic thought about a woman since you were in kindergarten." He turned to Brenna and said shortly, "This is Jake Dominic, Brenna."

Dominic glided forward, lithely graceful as a panther in pursuit of it's prey, to take her hand in his. He was almost sinfully handsome, she thought, with his dark eyes, dark hair, and the face of a fallen angel. If the eyes had the jaded cynicism of one who had done everything, seen everything, and found the world now a trifle boring, it only added to the wicked attraction of the man.

"You're always so gracious, Michael," he said over his shoulder, black eyes gleaming with amusement. Then he turned his attention to Brenna. His glance ran over her with lazy impudence. "Delightful, quite delightful!" he drawled softly. "It's really completely unfair of my barbaric friend here to try to keep such a prize to himself. I'm very happy to meet you, Miss Sloan."

"Cut it out, Jake," Donovan ordered bluntly. "What are you doing here? I told you this morning that I'd have Monty bring Brenna by the set tomorrow afternoon."

"I have to fly to Nevada in the morning to reshoot some scenes on location," Dominic said smoothly. "As you're so determined to have the picture finished on schedule, I thought I'd drop by and have my discussion with Miss Sloan tonight."

"At this time of night?" Donovan asked skeptically.

Dominic checked his watch casually. "It's barely eleven," he challenged. "Since when have you cared about keeping conventional hours where a picture is concerned?"

Donovan muttered a curse under his breath, and gave in abruptly. Turning to Brenna, his glance ran over her flimsily clad body critically. "Get dressed, Brenna," he ordered harshly.

An irrepressible chuckle escaped from Dominic, as the swift color came to Brenna's cheeks. With her head held high, she turned on her heel and strode furiously into the bedroom, slamming the door behind her.

As she quickly discarded the robe and donned panties and bra and a pair of faded blue jeans and a scarlet sweatshirt, she muttered stormy imprecations beneath her breath at the arrogance and chauvinism of men in general, and Donovan and Dominic in particular. Then putting her feet into a pair of scuffed loafers, she marched back into the living room. It did not improve her temper to see the two men apparently on the best of terms, drinks in their hands, talking in a desultory fashion about outtakes.

They both turned at her entrance, and a mischievous smile appeared on Dominic's face as he took in her less than elegant garb. "Ah, the young maid cometh," he said teasingly. "Tell me, Michael, do you think that outfit will sufficiently discourage my lustful nature?"

"Shut up, Jake," Donovan growled sourly.

Dominic cocked an eyebrow, dark eyes gleaming devilishly. "You know what a satyr I am," he said silkily. "I wonder if we should send over to wardrobe for a suit of armor."

"Jake!" Donovan said warningly.

"Or perhaps we could order a chastity belt," Dominic suggested irrepressibly.

"Very funny," Donovan said disgustedly.

"I thought so," Dominic said easily. "Now don't you think we've made Miss Sloan uncomfortable enough with our remarks? It's about time to get down to business. Run along, Michael, we have work to do."

A scowl darkened Michael's face. "I'm going to stay," he said belligerently.

Dominic raised his head, and suddenly the rakish playboy image was gone entirely. "No, you will not," he said sharply, dark eyes commanding. "We have a scene to go over. I have instructions to give, and a rapport to establish with an actress I'm directing in a film. I will not have you standing over us glowering like a jealous lover, and interfering with my work. You know damn well if you were directing, there's no way you would permit it. Well, neither will I!" He turned to Brenna and said in exasperation, "Will you kindly tell our mutual friend here that you're not afraid of the big bad wolf, and that he may leave with your sanction?"

Brenna was stunned at the amazing metamorphosis that had taken place before her eyes. Jake Dominic was obviously a very complex and powerful personality indeed to challenge a man of Donovan's calibre. "I'm not at all frightened of you, Mr. Dominic," she said slowly. "And Mr. Donovan knows very well that I don't want him here."

There was an incoherent exclamation

from Donovan as he slammed his drink down on the glass end table and strode angrily toward the door. Jerking it open, he turned to regard them grimly. "The only reason I'm leaving is because you're right, Jake. I'd react the same way to any interference while I was trying to do my job," he said harshly. "But you'd better be damn sure you stick to business!" The door slammed behind him with a resounding bang.

FIVE

Dominic flinched as he gazed at the still vibrating door. "I wonder just how close I was to being totally mangled," he mused.

"You didn't seem overly apprehensive," Brenna remarked dryly.

His expression was grim. "Don't kid yourself," he said bluntly. "One doesn't tease a grizzly bear without being fully conscious of the possible repercussions. You just have to weigh the values to be gained against the risks involved."

Brenna fastened on the simile. "A grizzly bear?" she asked curiously.

"Strong, powerful, 'the lord of the forest,' " he said, his gaze resting thoughtfully on her face. "How do you see him, Miss Sloan?"

She made a face. "If we're speaking of animals, I think you're completely mistaken; I see him as a cougar." She looked into Jake Dominic's eyes, and finished deliberately.

"And you as a black panther."

His lips quirked. "While you, without doubt, are a gazelle. Graceful, fragile, and the natural prey of either of us."

She continued to look at him steadily. "You forget that the gazelle is also very swift, Mr. Dominic. Given warning, I have no doubt I could elude destruction."

"The big cats give no warning, Miss Sloan," he replied softly. "Which is why you should realize you're wrong about Michael." His appraisal was coolly analytical.

"I would judge that in his usual blunt, bold fashion my red-haired friend has laid all his cards on the table. Michael has no use for subtleties."

Brenna blushed and lowered her eyes. "I've noticed that," she said ruefully.

Dominic looked down at his drink, a slight smile on his face. "I gather the gazelle is in full flight," he said lightly. "That's an unusual circumstance for Michael. It's no wonder he's in such a temper. He's definitely not used to being frustrated."

"Then he'll have to grow accustomed to it," Brenna said calmly.

There was a glimmer of admiration in Dominic's eyes as he looked up. "You know, it wasn't entirely business that prompted me to come here tonight," he said slowly.

"After I spoke to Michael this morning, I must admit to being intrigued. In all the years I've known Michael, he's never once warned me off a woman. I felt a certain curiosity to see the woman who had him in such turmoil. Now that I've seen you, I'm beginning to understand his predicament. You could be a very unsettling influence on a man, Miss Sloan."

"Does that mean you're going to ignore Donovan's warning, Mr. Dominic?" she asked challengingly.

His face was surprisingly serious as he shook his head. "Despite Michael's suspicious nature, I'm not about to set off in pursuit of you, charming though you may be," he said coolly. "I may be a thorough scoundrel and totally without scruples where women are concerned, but I place a great value on Michael's friendship." His eyes were half closed, as he continued almost beneath his breath, "I have no problem getting mistresses, but I doubt if I could replace Michael."

For a moment there was a curiously lonely and vulnerable look to his face, but it was quickly masked by cynicism. "So you see, you are in no danger where I'm concerned," he went on lightly. "I'm such a bastard that I can't afford to throw away lightly the few friends I have."

Brenna found herself suddenly liking this difficult, complex man. "I think you would make a very good friend," she said gently.

Dominic's brows shot up in surprise. "I don't believe a woman has ever told me that before," he said.

"I suppose they all just want you for your body?" Brenna said solemnly, her eyes twinkling.

"But of course," he said mournfully. "The heartless creatures persist in ignoring my brilliant mind and tortured soul." He pulled a face, and said melodramatically, "I'm only a sex object to them!"

Brenna chuckled, and they exchanged a glance that was suddenly free of tension. It was no wonder that he was such a heartbreaker, she thought in amusement. He moved from mood to mood with quicksilver rapidity, leaving one constantly off guard.

His black eyes were twinkling as he continued. "I'm really a closet virgin," he confided outrageously. "Please be gentle with me."

She shook her head, a slow smile curving her lips. "You're not at all what I expected, Mr. Dominic."

"Jake," he urged casually. "We're all on a first-name basis here." He put his glass on the table, and taking off his dark blue sports jacket, dropped it carelessly on the couch. "You're not what I expected either, Brenna," he said briskly. "Now, suppose you run along and get your script, and we'll get to work."

She found Dominic meant just that. For the next two hours there was no vestige of the personal in his demeanor. His manner was quick and incisive as they went over the role. With lightning verbal strokes he filled in the background she would need to fully understand the character: motivation, Mary's interaction and relationships with the other characters, and her own role as a catalyst in the story line.

After the preliminary discussions were over, he had her read through the script, stopping her frequently to explain a point or correct her interpretation of a line. Then he had her go through it again without interruption, watching her with a quiet intensity that she found to be both soothing and stimulating.

When she had finished, he leaned back lazily on the couch and regarded her thoughtfully through half-closed lids.

"You have a quick, intelligent mind, Brenna," he said quietly. "I rather think you're one of those people who never makes the same mistake twice."

Brenna knew a swift rush of pleasure at his obvious approval. She could see why Jake was considered so exceptional. It was incredible that in such a short time he had accomplished so much. She not only felt she understood the character in depth, but he had mysteriously instilled in her both enthusiasm and confidence.

"Thank you, Jake," she said sincerely. "You've made it very easy for me."

"My pleasure, believe me," he said with a grin. "Though Michael doesn't usually let his personal feelings influence his judgment, I confess that I was afraid you might be the horrible exception. I had visions of trying to mold an actress out of some stagestruck ingenue." His face darkened. "God knows, we have had enough problems with this picture."

"Mary Durney was supposed to be played by Tammy Silvers, wasn't she?" Brenna asked curiously. "I read that she won a Tony Award last year for *Little Sins.*"

Dominic nodded, his lips thin. "She had excellent credentials, and she looked the part," he said shortly. "But she began to believe her own press clippings."

Seeing Brenna's still-puzzled face, he continued briefly, "Temperament on the set, skipped wardrobe fittings, tardiness. She was a real bitch."

"She had a contract, didn't she?" Brenna asked. "How did you get around that?"

He smiled with feral satisfaction. "Donovan insists on a clause in all performer's contracts that permits dismissal if the actor proves unsatisfactory at any time."

Brenna's eyes widened. "Isn't that rather unusual?" she asked, startled.

"The option is very seldom exercised," he said coolly. "Donovan may create stars, but he won't tolerate a performer behaving like one." His mouth twisted wryly. "He has no need to. Unknowns and stars alike stand in line to be in a Donovan Ltd. film."

Brenna nodded slowly, knowing this was true.

For the next twenty minutes they discussed the difference between stage and film work, Dominic outlining clearly the techniques and skills the medium would demand of her.

When he finally rose to go, her head was whirling with information that he had fed her with computer-like efficiency. Shrugging into his jacket, he smoothed his rumpled black hair quickly, and turned back to Brenna with an easy smile. "I think we've covered everything," he said slowly. "I'll be back late tomorrow evening, so we won't begin work until day after tomorrow. Report to makeup at 6 a.m."

As she rose and accompanied him to the door, his eyes took in the confusion on her face with a compassionate understanding that she would never have believed he possessed two hours ago.

"It will all come together," he said quietly, as he opened the door. "Trust me. I promise that you will be a great Mary Durney." He continued teasingly, "How could you help it with such a brilliant director?"

She smiled. "You're right, how could I help it?" she echoed valiantly. "Good night, Jake. You've been super. How can I ever thank you?"

His dark eyes twinkled wickedly. "If I wasn't on my best behavior, I'd tell you explicitly," he said with a wide grin. "But as I am walking the path of virtue, I can only beg you not to let it get around that I spent two hours alone with you without making a single pass. It would ruin my reputation!"

"It'll be our secret," Brenna assured him gravely.

As the door closed behind him with a soft click, she leaned against it for a moment, smiling softly. The past two hours had instilled in her a buoyant confidence in her abilities that she had never known before.

She was suddenly blissfully certain that everything was going to work out to her complete satisfaction.

The panicky urge to bolt and run that had possessed her after the passionate interlude with Donovan had gradually faded as the evening progressed. Why should she give up an opportunity that could mean financial security for Randy, and a fantastic start in her chosen profession just because Michael Donovan had decided she was to be his next mistress? The decision was not solely his, she thought defiantly, as she flicked off the lights on the way to the bedroom. She had fended off the most intricate of passes from men who thought she was easy game. She would handle Donovan with the same cool aloofness. Hadn't he promised there would be no confrontation till the picture was finished? It should be a simple matter to see that she was safely out of his reach when the time came.

As for his intention to wear down her resistance before then, she doubted that he would have the opportunity from what Jake Dominic had told her about her proposed schedule. It was going to be nonstop work from now until the final scene was shot. And if Donovan valued his precious timetable as much as he appeared to, he would have to leave her alone to get on with it.

Brenna was determined that he would find her much less compliant at their next encounter. It must have been surprise, coupled with Donovan's undoubted sexual expertise, that had reduced her to such a state of almost abject desire, she thought firmly. Now that she was on guard, she would see that no break in her armor would allow him a similar advantage.

With this firm resolution in mind, she quickly unpacked her bags, and put away her clothes. They filled only one bureau drawer and not even a quarter of the closet space. It was obvious that the residents of these luxurious cottages were expected to possess a far more extensive wardrobe than she did, she thought ruefully. She shrugged philosophically. She had not come here to model clothes but to act, and after Jake Dominic's encouragement this evening, she had every confidence that she could perform that function with a large degree of success.

After brushing her teeth, setting her alarm, and donning her very utilitarian cotton pajamas, she slipped between the cream satin sheets, feeling very much the plain brown wren in this lush Sybarite nest. Weary as she was, it was still a long time before her adrenaline-charged mind gave in to the demands of her exhausted body. Her thoughts were a wildly confused kaleidoscope that whirled in erratic circles over the feverish events of the last two days. It seemed impossible that a person's life could change with such speed. Not only her physical surroundings, but the inhabitants of her new world were strange and exotic, and she felt suddenly very unsure and alone.

But she wasn't alone, she assured herself steadily. She still had Randy, even though he wasn't in her immediate vicinity. She had not given up her determination to change that status as soon as possible. She would find a way to circumvent Donovan's ridiculous orders at the first opportunity. In the meantime, she would focus her thoughts on Randy, the only dear, familiar object in this frightening world. Gradually, as she did this, she was filled with the accustomed warm serenity, and she became drowsy and relaxed.

Yet it wasn't Randy's golden hair and puckish smile that was her last vision before she dropped off to sleep, but the blunt, rugged features and dark red hair of Michael Donovan.

Even though the following day was jam-packed with activity, Brenna was to look on it later as being positively leisurely. The morning was spent memorizing her lines, with special emphasis on the scenes Dominic had indicated he wanted her to concentrate on for the following day. She blessed the fact that she was the quick study that Wilkes had bragged about. By noon she had the scenes learned to her satisfaction, though she knew she would have to refresh her memory each day before going to the set. One of the advantages of work in films was obviously going to be the convenience of focusing one's efforts on one or two scenes a day and not to have to worry about the production as a whole. Whether this would prove an asset in the long run was debatable, she thought skeptically. She knew she was one of those performers who could lose herself in the role when involved in the continuity of an actual play. Whether this magic could occur when she was faced with doing one isolated scene after another in disjointed sequence, she had no way of knowing.

At lunchtime she hurried to Doris Charles' apartment to check on Randy. Donovan had not exaggerated, she discovered when she let herself in at Doris Charles' shouted invitation. Randy had every possible necessity and amusement to keep the most pampered child in ecstasy. He greeted her with his usual cheerful ebullience and then ignored her and went back to painstakingly linking a caboose to the cars of a brightly painted wooden train.

Doris, dressed in jeans and a plaid shirt, was sitting cross-legged on the floor beside him. She looked up with a wide grin as Brenna entered.

"Hi," she said cheerfully. "This young man of yours is on his way to becoming a railroad tycoon. Before we're done, we may stretch from coast to coast. Care to join us?"

Brenna shook her head, her gaze lingering on the chubby romper-clad figure. "I only have a minute," she said wistfully. "I just stopped to make sure that he was all right. Did he sleep well?"

"Like a top," the nurse said serenely. "And he ate a breakfast this morning that would do justice to a lumberjack. I haven't been able to pry him away from all these toys, but as soon as he loses interest, I'll take him down to the pool to get some sun."

"He'll love that," Brenna said smiling. "He's a real water baby."

"I noticed that last night when I gave him his bath," Doris said wryly. "He nearly drowned me!"

Brenna chuckled understandingly. "I've

113

often been tempted to change into a bikini before tackling that particular job," she admitted.

"Hey! I may just try that," the nurse said, eyes twinkling. "Provided I survive our dip in the pool this afternoon." Her gray eyes were kind as she went on gently. "It's always difficult when a mother is separated from her child for the first time. I want you to know that I'm taking the very best care of Randy, and he's adjusting very well."

There was a suspicious moisture in Brenna's eyes and she blinked rapidly. "I'm sure he's doing a good deal better than I am," she said huskily. "He's had considerable experience."

"He's a perfect angel," Doris said enthusiastically. "I'm going to miss him like crazy when this job is finished." She cocked a sandy eyebrow quizzically. "You wouldn't need a permanent nanny by any chance?"

Brenna shook her head. "I'm afraid I couldn't afford you. I'm only just getting started. It will be some time before I can think about employing someone with your qualifications."

The nurse shrugged. "You never can tell," she said easily. "Keep me in mind, if your ship comes in."

Brenna nodded. "I'll do that," she replied

lightly. She kissed Randy quickly, and then said reluctantly, "I have to leave now. Someone is waiting for me. I'll try to get back this evening in time for his dinner."

"Fine," Doris said cheerfully. "Whenever you have a little extra time, just call, and I'll bring Randy down to the cottage. I'll always advise reception where we are, if we leave the apartment."

Brenna felt a little pang at the nurse's attitude, as if it were the most common thing in the world for a mother to make an appointment to see her own son. She smothered the illogical feeling at once. It didn't make sense to harbor such envy against Doris. She was a warm, competent person, and evidently got along famously with Randy. She was making the situation as easy as possible under the circumstances.

This didn't prevent Brenna from feeling a trifle dejected as she went to the cafeteria. She joined Monty, who poured her a cup of coffee from the carafe on the table. He watched silently as she absently took a sip, grimaced, and then reached for the cream.

"Something wrong?" he asked with a frown.

Brenna shook her head. "Not really. I'm just suffering withdrawal pains," she said with forced cheerfulness. "Randy is having himself a ball."

There was frank relief in Walters' face, as he said heartily, "That's great! Mr. Donovan told me this morning before he left that I was to make sure you weren't worrying about the kid."

"Mr. Donovan has gone?" Brenna asked slowly, wondering why the news didn't bring the expected relief. After keying herself up in anticipation of an encounter with the man, she felt a real letdown when she realized her efforts had been totally unnecessary.

"He flew to London this morning," Walters said casually. "There's some special effects genius he wants to recruit for the science fiction picture he's planning for next spring."

"When will he be back?" Brenna asked, looking down at her coffee, her lashes veiling the interest in her eyes.

Walters shrugged. "Who knows? He has interests all over the world besides Donovan Ltd." He glanced at his watch hurriedly. "I hate to rush you, Brenna, but you have an appointment with Simon Burke, Donovan's attorney, to sign your contract in fifteen minutes."

Brenna pushed her cup away, and rose to her feet. "Then let's go," she said cheerfully.

The rest of the day passed with the flickering acceleration of an old silent movie. After the contract was signed, Monty escorted her to wardrobe, where she was fitted for the outfits she was to wear in the scenes the following day. From there she was whirled to publicity where she gave a brief synopsis of her background, and was assigned an appointment to have still photographs taken for the publicity releases.

"I'll keep in touch," Monty promised, as he let Brenna out at her cottage that evening. "Let me know if there's anything you need," he said cheerfully. "And don't let Dominic work you too hard. He has the reputation of being something of a slave driver."

In the weeks to come she was to look back with grim amusement at that warning from Walters. She soon discovered that she had as much chance of following that advice as to change the path of a hurricane. Jake Dominic trampled over obstacles as if they did not exist. In his ruthless drive for perfection, he spared neither himself, his crew, nor the cast. Brenna found herself on an exhausting merry-go-round from six in the morning till eight in the evening, and sometimes even later.

Then she would hurry home and spend a

few precious moments with Randy, before settling down to work on her lines and blocking for the next day's shooting. If the pace had not been so killing, she would have enjoyed the filming itself. All the members of the cast and the crew had a friendly professionalism that made them a pleasure to work with. And if Dominic was demanding, he was also both stimulating and inspirational. There was no limit to the help and time he was willing to extend to get the results he wanted. Her admiration for his ingenuity and directorial genius grew with every passing day, as the pressure mounted and Dominic labored to bring the film in on schedule.

Because most of the scenes still to be completed were those that had to be reshot with Brenna replacing Tammy Silvers, Dominic's demands were focused almost exclusively on Brenna. When she arrived back at the cottage, she was too weary to do anything but go over her lines and then fall into bed in total exhaustion. She was often too tired to bother to eat, and, always slim and fragile looking, her appearance soon became positively ethereal.

It was this fact that caused Dominic's tightly leashed temper to explode one morning with all the accompanying fireworks, just two days before production was due to be completed.

They had barely begun shooting that morning when he called a strident "cut." He strode angrily toward Brenna, his face darkening ominously. "Wardrobe!" he bellowed furiously. "Dammit, get me someone from wardrobe! What the hell are they trying to do to me?"

Brenna stared at him in confusion as he took her by the shoulders and spun her around swiftly, cursing steadily beneath his breath. "My God! They've made you into a damn caricature!"

Sandra Stafford, the dark, plump wardrobe mistress, scurried hurriedly onto the set, her eyes anxiously fixed on Dominic's angry face. "Mrs. Stafford," Dominic said sarcastically, "perhaps you weren't aware that Miss Sloan is not supposed to be a holocaust survivor from a concentration camp, but a cosseted daughter of an affluent family." His hand tugged angrily at a loose fold of material. "In short, Mrs. Stafford, her gowns are supposed to fit!"

The wardrobe mistress stared in horror at Brenna's green gown. Though Dominic's condemnation had been exaggerated, the gown was undoubtedly ill-fitting and cumbersome looking.

She cast a frightened look at Dominic's forbidding countenance and said nervously, "I'm terribly sorry, Mr. Dominic. We'll correct it right away."

"In the interim the entire cast and crew sit around cooling their heels," he said caustically.

A flush of anger tinted Sandra Stafford's cheeks pink, as she answered defensively. "I said I was sorry, Mr. Dominic, but it's not really wardrobe's fault. That gown was a perfect fit when we made the final alterations four days ago. Miss Sloan must have lost weight."

"She's right, Jake," Brenna put in quickly. "The dress did fit on Tuesday."

Dominic's displeasure was immediately directed toward Brenna. Turning his back on the relieved wardrobe mistress, his dark eyes went over Brenna critically. "For God's sake, Brenna, you must have lost ten pounds in the last three weeks," he said explosively, his black eyes flaming. "How irresponsible can you get! Didn't it occur to you that your appearance can't change from scene to scene?"

Brenna could feel the humiliating color rise in her face at this public denunciation. She raised her chin defiantly. "I didn't do it on purpose," she defended herself. "It just happened."

"A stroke of fate, perhaps," Jake said with intimidating softness. "Mother nature waves her magic wand, and you lose ten pounds."

"I may have missed a few meals," Brenna stammered uncomfortably.

"She skipped a few meals," he said sarcastically. "May we inquire how many?"

"I don't remember," Brenna said defensively, becoming angry in her turn. Surely this castigation wasn't necessary. "I told you I didn't do it deliberately."

"Leave her alone, Jake," Michael Donovan said lazily.

They both turned in surprise, squinting against the glare of the lights to see Donovan's familiar figure leaning indolently against a pillar in the far corner of the sound stage. Donovan's red hair burned like a dark flame in the dimness of the shadows as he straightened, and strolled causally forward. He was dressed informally, as usual, in a cinnamon brown shirt and fitted khaki slacks that explicitly molded the strong lines of his thighs.

"Well, well," Dominic drawled sardonically, "the wanderer returns. When did you get home?"

"Last night," Donovan said laconically.

She had forgotten how piercing those blue

eyes were, Brenna thought with a shiver, as his mocking gaze examined her face with a familiar intimacy.

"Hello, Brenna," he said softly.

"Good morning, Mr. Donovan," she said with a composure she didn't really feel. It was only the surprise of seeing him so unexpectedly that caused that tingling warmth in her veins, she told herself stubbornly.

Donovan raised an eyebrow quizzically at her formality, and turned to Dominic. "You're in a foul mood, Jake," he drawled. "I can't see that Brenna's done anything to deserve that serpent's tongue of yours. You've obviously been working the girl to a shadow. You're going to have more problems than a few pounds weight loss if you don't let up. She looks almost breakable."

"I'm quite well, Mr. Donovan," Brenna said coolly.

To her annoyance both men blatantly ignored the interruption. "My God, Michael!" Dominic said harshly. "I have a picture to finish. What do you want me to do, set up banker's hours for the girl? You're the one who gave me the deadline for this film. Now it's my job to try and meet it."

"You're quite right, I did set the deadline," Donovan said coolly. "And I'm the one who can change it. Brenna needs a rest. Schedule her out of the shooting today."

Brenna's eyes widened with shock, and she opened her mouth to protest, but Dominic was before her.

"Schedule her out of . . ." he repeated dumbfounded, then continued explosively, "And what do you suggest we do while Miss Sloan 'rests'?"

Donovan shrugged. "Shoot around her, or give everyone a day's rest. You decide, Jake," he said carelessly. "But make up your mind that whatever you do today, it's not going to involve Brenna."

With a firm hand on her elbow he half led, half pushed Brenna ahead of him off the set, past the gaping crew, toward the door that led to the parking lot.

"What are you doing?" she hissed furiously. "There's absolutely nothing wrong with me, and I have no intention of going anywhere with you!"

"Be quiet, sweetheart," Donovan said serenely. "You're going to do exactly what you're told, for once."

"For once?" Brenna sputtered indignantly. "You've done nothing but order me around since the moment we met, Michael Donovan, and I have yet to get my own way."

Donovan's blue eyes gleamed mischievously. "But then, neither have I, love," he drawled meaningfully.

Brenna blushed fiercely, and tried futilely to wrest her arm from Donovan's iron grip, as they reached the door. "You can't come in here and just whisk me away, without so much as a by your leave to anyone," she protested. "And just look at me. I've got to return this gown to wardrobe!"

He pushed her through the door, and strode quickly toward a sleek gray Mercedes, dragging Brenna along behind him.

"I can do anything I want to do," he said coolly. "I own the place, remember? As for the gown, we'll stop at your cottage and you can change. I'll send someone over to pick it up after we leave."

"Leave? Where are we going?" Brenna squeaked. "Wasn't the entire purpose of this abduction so that I could get some rest?"

"Certainly," Donovan agreed blandly. "And I fully intend that you do just that. Which doesn't necessarily mean that I'm ordering you to bed —" he grinned innocently, "— at the moment." He opened the passenger door and seated her carefully before closing the door and running around to slip behind the wheel. "I'm taking you away from all this, brown eyes," he grated, in a passable Bogart imitation.

"And what if I don't want to be taken away?" Brenna asked archly, trying to smother the fugitive amusement that this new, lighthearted Donovan produced. How many facets were there to Donovan's complicated personality, she wondered helplessly. Each encounter with this human dynamo left her struggling helplessly out of her depth.

He started the motor, but did not put the car into gear. He turned to face her, his expression serious. "You need a break, Brenna," he said quietly, his fingers lightly tracing the faint shadows beneath her eyes that even makeup had not been able to cover entirely. "Jake may be a cinematic genius, but he'll ride roughshod over anything that gets in his way. I'd forgotten you were so vulnerable, or I wouldn't have stayed away so long." His tone was infinitely gentle, his eyes enfolding her in a flowering warmth that could be tenderness.

Brenna caught her breath, and forced herself to look away before that gaze completely dissolved any resistance she could muster to Donovan's powerful charisma. "I'm really quite all right," she insisted shakily. "I'm much tougher than I look."

His hand reached out to encircle one fragile wrist, and she jumped involuntarily at the sensation that passed through her at his casual touch.

"I have no doubt you have the heart of a lion," he said lightly. "But it's obvious that your physical stamina doesn't match up. A puff of wind could blow you away." His eyes darkened angrily. "What the hell could Jake have been thinking of to let you get in this shape?"

A sudden poignant warmth shot through Brenna, melting any remaining resistance. It had been so long since she had had anyone to worry about her physical well-being, she thought mistily. Not since Janine had died, had anyone expressed any personal concern for her. Even with Janine it had been she and not her older sister who was the caretaker. Thinking back, Brenna couldn't remember anyone who had given her this wonderful, comforting feeling of being treasured. She felt a sudden urge to surrender, to throw off the burden of independence and responsibility that seemed too heavy to bear, to lean on Donovan's vibrant strength that she knew would so effortlessly shield her. She knew this mood wouldn't last; soon her independence would reassert itself, and she would once again be ready to do battle in the arena. But not now. She was so tired. Surely it wouldn't hurt to lay aside her armor for just a little while and be young and carefree.

She turned once again to meet his eyes and asked quietly, "So what do you suggest?"

"I have a cottage on a tiny island just off the coast," he said, his narrowed eyes on her face, weighing her every reaction. "We can be there by helicopter in an hour. It's quite beautiful and very peaceful. No telephone, no television, and no Jake Dominic to intrude on your rest. I promise to have you back in your own chaste little cottage before sunset."

"You make it sound very appealing," Brenna said slowly. It sounded like paradise, she thought longingly.

Donovan's rapier eyes read the wistfulness in her face, and he moved in with swift aggression. "I'm not about to rape you, if that's what you're worried about," he said bluntly. "I would hardly incur the expense of a full day of lost production, just to get you into bed. That would make you very expensive, indeed. I don't promise not to try to make love to you, but it will be you that sets the pace. All you have to do is say 'no.' "

"I'll go," she said recklessly.

An almost boyish smile lit Donovan's rugged features. "Great," he said tersely, and putting the car in gear, he backed out of the parking space and drove rapidly out of the lot.

Six

The whir of the scarlet helicopter's rotors died to a whisper, and Donovan reached across to unsnap Brenna's seat belt with swift economical movements. "Stay where you are," he ordered briskly. "I'll come around and help you down."

Brenna nodded absently, as she peered eagerly through the window at the small clearing surrounded by towering pines. They had landed on a square concrete landing pad, and she watched impatiently as Donovan attached lines to the helicopter from steel links embedded in the concrete. He paused to look speculatively at the darkening sky to the west, before coming around to the door and opening it.

"Looks like we're going to get a bit of a storm," he said, as he reached up and, placing his two hands firmly on her waist, swung her easily to the ground. "I was hoping the weather would be good, so that we could go out in the boat," he said frowning. "Are you a sailor, Brenna?"

"I have no idea," she said simply. "I've never been on a boat."

She had said the same thing about flying, when they had arrived at the private landing strip on the outskirts of Twin Pines a little over an hour ago.

Shutting the helicopter door, Donovan took her hand in his and set off up the pebbled path that led across the clearing, into the dense stand of trees.

"I have an idea a man could become addicted to providing you with new experiences, Brenna Sloan," he said thoughtfully. "It would give him a never-ending source of pleasure."

She made a face, as she gave a half skip to keep up with his lengthy stride. "Where were you ten years ago?" she asked lightly. "Orphanage brats lead notoriously dull lives."

His hand tightened protectively around hers. He didn't look at her as he asked quietly, "Was it very bad, Brenna?"

"The children's home?" She shook her head. "No, not really bad," she said matter of factly. "Lonely, sometimes."

They had reached the glade now, and Brenna cocked an eyebrow inquiringly.

"Would it be too much to ask where we're going?"

"The cabin is about a quarter of a mile from here," he said. "I thought we'd stop there first to take some steaks out of the freezer, before we take a hike around the island." His eyes appraised the horizon critically. "It looks like the storm may hold off for a while. It's moving slowly."

After that, they moved in companionable silence through the woods. Brenna breathed in the pine-scented, pungent air with warm contentment. For a city bred person like herself this simple walk through the woods had all the attraction of the exotic. She was as lighthearted and happy as a child at this moment, and a great part of it was due to this man, who was holding her hand with such casual camaraderie.

From the moment she had agreed to come to Donovan's island, he had been everything one could have wished in a companion. He had carefully kept any sign of sexual awareness from his attitude during the time he had driven her to the cottage, and waited while she quickly changed into white shorts, sneakers, and a yellow sun top. She had washed the heavy makeup off and hadn't bothered to replace it, relying on the glowing perfection of her healthy skin. She had hurriedly brushed out the elaborate hairdo, letting her hair fall in its usual gleaming curtain down her back. Then they had hurried like two eager schoolchildren to the airstrip to board the helicopter. Somehow it did not surprise her at all that Donovan could pilot the helicopter himself, and was also licensed to fly the Lear jet that was hangared at the field. A man as dominant as Donovan would want to be fully in command, wherever he was.

They had been walking for about five minutes and Brenna could see the outline of the redwood chalet in a distant clearing. She asked curiously, "Don't you find such a totally isolated hideaway inconvenient? I should think you would at least want a telephone to keep in contact with your business interests."

Donovan shook his head decisively. "No way!" he said curtly. "I bought the island two years ago for the express purpose of having a place to go when I wanted to do some writing. I wouldn't get anything accomplished if I could be reached by phone. If anything urgent comes up, Monty can always hire a helicopter or a launch to bring him over."

They had reached the clearing now, and Brenna saw the A-frame chalet. The cabin, while charming, was really quite small. When she commented on this, Donovan smiled, his blue eyes dancing.

"It was quite large enough for the original owner's purpose," he said dryly. "I bought it from one of Dominic's playboy buddies, who had it built to his own specifications."

Suspecting that she knew the answer already, she asked, "And that purpose was?"

"A love nest," he said succinctly.

"I see," Brenna said thoughtfully, her eyes gleaming curiously, a question trembling on her lips.

"And, no, I have never used the cabin for that reason." He anticipated her question with a grin. "I come here to work."

Donovan unlocked the door and, with a mocking gesture, indicated that she should precede him, then followed her closely so that he could see her reaction. He wasn't disappointed.

Brenna gazed around as wide-eyed as a child. A love nest, indeed, she thought faintly. The chalet had a floor plan that provided no privacy whatever. The living room area flowed into the tiny kitchenette with only the free-style cabinets to divide the room. A spiral staircase led to a half-loft that was occupied by a king-sized bed and two bedside tables. The decor was contemporary, with the accent on comfort, and sang with glowing reds and orange. A huge stone fireplace dominated one wall, with a long, scarlet couch and a white fur rug placed cozily before it. There was an almost overpoweringly intimate atmosphere about the chalet, and she was filled with a strange tension under Donovan's mocking stare.

"What, no communal bathing?" Brenna asked jokingly, her eyes not meeting his.

"Now that you mention it," he said lazily, and sauntering over to the far wall, he slid a decorative panel aside to reveal an enormous emerald green sunken tub, surrounded by several white potted ferns.

"The poor fellow was painfully obvious, wasn't he?" Donovan commented casually. "One hopes his little playmates came here with the same aim in view. One look at this setup would send any shrinking violet running for the hills screaming bloody murder."

He slid the screen closed, and, ignoring Brenna's scarlet face, strode quickly to the tiny kitchen. Rummaging in the compact freezer, he triumphantly extracted two paper-wrapped packages and put them in the portable microwave, pushing the button to defrost.

"All set," he announced crisply, coming around the counter into the living room area. "Shall we go?"

Brenna nodded quickly, and hurried out the door and down the steps, conscious all the time of Donovan's amusement. Once outside, she breathed a covert sigh of relief, and, turning to Donovan, asked eagerly, "Where shall we go?"

He smiled indulgently at the glowing eagerness on her face. "I thought we'd climb the hill and watch the storm approach. It can be quite an experience. Would you like that?"

"I'd love it," Brenna said enthusiastically, her brown eyes shining.

"You're easily pleased," Donovan said dryly, as he took her hand once more, and they set off toward the hill he had indicated. "The last time I saw that much enthusiasm on a woman's face, she'd just been gifted with a diamond bracelet."

"By you, no doubt," Brenna said lightly, ignoring the twinge she experienced at the intimacy implied in Donovan's comment. She was determined to let nothing spoil this day. "How cynical you and Jake are about women. There are a few women in the world who aren't for sale, you know."

Donovan's hand tightened painfully on hers, but his voice was even as he said carefully, "You appear to have a fairly intimate

135

knowledge of Jake's attitudes. Could it be that Jake has been up to his usual shenanigans?"

For a moment she was tempted to lie, to see if she could break the tight control on Donovan's face, but then she discarded the impulse. She wanted no tension to destroy the harmony of the moment. She shook her head. "Nope," she said matter-of-factly, making a face. "The only interest your charming friend has in me is purely analytical. He wants to see how hard he can push me before I collapse."

Donovan's grip relaxed fractionally. "And I'll lay odds he'll probably be there with open arms to catch you when you do," he said dryly.

Brenna giggled helplessly, as she suddenly had a mental picture of a villainous Dominic, complete with moustache and flowing cape, clutching her in a Valentino-style embrace.

A smile tugged at the corners of Donovan's lips at the contagious quality of her mirth.

"I'm glad you find the idea so amusing," he said lightly. "I assure you that is not the usual feminine reaction to Jake."

She tossed her head, tilting her nose saucily. "I've come to the conclusion that you

136

both take yourselves far too seriously," she said sweetly, as they started up the twisted dirt path that led to the top of the hill. "It's about time someone took you down a peg."

Donovan cocked an eyebrow. "You're feeling brave today, aren't you, sweetheart?" he murmured softly. "That wouldn't be in the nature of a dare, would it?"

She backed down hurriedly, at the dangerous glint in his blue eyes. "You and Jake have been friends for a long time, haven't you?" she asked quickly, hoping to distract him.

There was a short silence before Donovan accused softly, "Chicken! I'll let you escape this time, but don't issue challenges unless you're prepared to follow through, Brenna." He watched with amusement as color flooded her cheeks, before he took pity on her. "In answer to your question, Jake and I have been friends since college. We both attended UCLA." He grimaced wryly. "Not that we moved in the same circles. I was a slum kid working my way through by doing construction work on the side, and Jake was heir to Dominic's Shipping — the original golden boy." The look in Donovan's eyes was far away as he murmured, "We were a mismatched pair. God knows why we didn't hate each other. I was a defensive young tough with a king-sized chip on my shoulder, and Jake was a hell-raising bastard who didn't give a damn about anyone. We were at each other's throats constantly, until we found we had one thing in common that made all our differences minute in comparison. We both felt that film-making was the ultimate art form, and we were both determined to make the best damn pictures in the history of the business."

"You had one other thing in common," Brenna said teasingly. "What about your overwhelming modesty?"

Donovan grinned in acknowledgment of the gentle thrust. "Neither of us was ever bothered with an excess of that virtue," he admitted simply. "We always knew what we could do."

Yes, there would never be any doubt in Donovan's mind about his own abilities, she thought, as she stared with new eyes at the powerful body and bold features of the man. Before this she had looked upon him as some sort of super being, sprung fully grown, with the faculty to mold and disrupt her life.

He had unbuttoned his cotton shirt to the waist as they had started their climb, and her eyes were drawn in fascination to the strong shoulders and chest muscles with the dark red patch of wiry hair that narrowed to a fine line as it approached the waistband of his slacks. Those muscles had been formed by hard physical labor on innumerable construction sites, as a young boy struggled desperately to overcome his background and get a decent education. If he was arrogant and cynical, wasn't it a natural byproduct of the struggle to survive and reach the dizzy heights which he was innately conscious were his destiny?

"Do you have a family?" she asked, suddenly wanting to know more of the past that had created Michael Donovan.

He shrugged, his face closed. "My mother died when I was twelve. I guess I still have a father wandering around someplace. I really wouldn't know. I ran away from home when I was fourteen."

They crested the hill suddenly, and Brenna drew in her breath sharply at the sight that almost physically assaulted her senses. Gone was the gentle terrain with a dramatic abruptness that was overpowering in its impact. The summit fell away to the sea far below in a sheer drop, and there was nothing before them but an endless stretch of sea and sky. At first glance it seemed that the two were one vast seething entity. The storm was moving swiftly now. The churning cobalt of the waves mirrored the ominous force of the clouds, as the quickening wind strived to bind the dichotomy into a tumultuous whole.

"It's magnificent!" Brenna breathed, awestruck, as she moved irresistibly closer to the edge of the cliff in an unconscious desire to become part of the raw, elemental savagery that was swiftly surrounding them.

"It will be on us in a few moments," Donovan observed. "If you don't want to get half drowned, we should start back right away."

She shook off his restraining hand and stepped closer to the edge. "I've never seen anything like this," she murmured ecstatically. The temperature had dropped at least ten degrees in the last few minutes, and the wind that stung her face and caused her hair to billow out behind her in a wild banner was almost cold.

Donovan let her go, his eyes narrowed and watchful, but not interfering with the emotional response that the storm had stirred in her.

Suddenly they were enveloped in the mysterious golden twilight that preceded the unleashing of the storm. Donovan felt compelled to issue a final warning, which he already knew would be futile by the rapt fascination on Brenna's face.

He was right. She didn't even look at him as she replied absently, "You go on ahead. I'll be along later."

His mouth twisted in amused resignation, and leaning casually against a boulder a little distance away from the figure on the headland, he crossed his arms and prepared to wait.

He didn't have to wait long. The golden twilight faded to violet dimness and the distant growling of the thunder became a savage roar as the heavens exploded, and sheets of rain whipped at them with savage fury.

The exultant oneness with nature that Brenna was feeling was magnified rather than diminished by the pouring rain that completely drenched them in a matter of moments. A cold wind tore at her hair and clothes like a ravening animal. She opened her mouth to let the drops caress her lips, and stretched out her arms in supplication and embrace. She was conscious of the smallness and fragility of each separate limb and muscle of her body, and at the same time she felt as strong and powerful as a goddess from Olympus.

She laughed exultantly, glancing at Donovan's watchful face as she tossed back her sodden hair from her face, still holding her arms before her like a high priestess invoking the fury of the storm. "I'm going to live forever, Donovan!" she shouted triumphantly. "Do you hear me? I'm going to live forever!"

There was a tolerant smile on Donovan's face as he levered himself away from the boulder, and lazily crossed to stand beside her. He, too, was soaked, his shirt and trousers plastered to his muscular body like a second skin, his hair rain-darkened to almost black.

He took her elbow and propelled her firmly away from the edge of the cliff. "You're not even going to live till next week, if you catch a chill from this drenching, you crazy woman," he said roughly. "Your skin is as cold as ice."

"I'm not cold. I feel wonderful. I feel terrific," she said giddily. "I've never felt so alive in my life."

"Yes, I know. You're going to live forever," he said dryly. "But right now you're going to jog back to the cabin to get your circulation working."

With a hand on her elbow, he set the pace and they were soon half running, half sliding down the hill. The dirt path was now a muddy quagmire, and it was almost impossible to keep one's footing. Several times Brenna found herself sitting ingloriously in the mud, the rain pouring over her in buckets while she collapsed in helpless laughter. In this crazy exultant mood, she could take nothing seriously. It was a moment out of time, to be enjoyed and savored to the hilt.

Each time she fell, Donovan picked her up patiently, shaking his head ruefully at her giddiness and urging her on with quiet determination. Once they reached the bottom of the hill, the going was easier, and it was only a matter of minutes before they were running up the steps to the chalet. They were both breathing hard from the run, but as Brenna leaned back against the door, she felt no weariness, only happiness and a bubbling confidence in herself and the world around her. After the countless days of pressure, she was drunk on the sheer exhilaration of being joyfully alive.

She looked blithely around the chalet. It no longer intimidated, but merely amused her. Donovan himself was a far from intimidating figure, sopping wet and woefully mud splattered.

"What would everyone say if they could see the big movie tycoon now?" she giggled irrepressibly.

"They'd say he looked a great deal better than a certain fledgling actress," he said coolly, shaking his head. Brenna's shorts and top were wet and clinging to her slim body, her long, wet hair hanging in ropy strands around her glowing face. "And you're still cold," he went on briskly, as he touched her throat lightly. With swift strides he crossed the room to the portable bar at one side of the stone fireplace, and poured something dark and potent looking into a glass. He returned to offer it to her commandingly.

"Drink it all," he ordered curtly. "It will warm you."

She started to protest that she didn't need warming, but one look at his determined face convinced her that it would be useless. She drained the glass in one swallow and collapsed against the door, gasping, her face a bright scarlet.

"For God's sake, that was straight whiskey," Donovan said impatiently. "You're supposed to sip it, not gulp it."

"How was I supposed to know that?" she wheezed, her eyes tearing. "I've never had whiskey before."

"Another famous first," he said ironically. "Sit down while I see if I can scare up something for you to change into." Not waiting for her reply, he took the spiral steps to the sleeping area two at a time.

She obediently headed toward the scarlet velvet couch, but looking ruefully down at her dripping form, she moved instead to lean against the fireplace. Now that the first violent effects of the whiskey were over, she found that the liquor did make her feel warmer, and what was more, it increased the delicious euphoria that she was experiencing. She was delighted that the whiskey seemed to have no other effect on her, and she impulsively moved to the liquor cabinet and poured herself another. This time she did sip it more cautiously, but found that it still gave her that all-pervading sensation of well-being. She was just about to refill her glass again, when Donovan returned with an armful of clothes and two fluffy white towels. He arched his brows inquiringly, as he looked pointedly at the glass in her hand.

"I've decided I like it," she announced cheerfully, smiling at him. "I must have a good head for liquor. It has practically no effect on me at all."

"Amazing," he drawled mockingly, as he firmly took the glass from her, and set it on the bar. He placed the clothes and towels in her arms, and, strolling over to the ornamental screen, drew it aside and turned on the faucets full force in the sunken tub.

"Get undressed, and into that tub," he ordered briskly. "I'll light a fire, and then put on the steaks."

She stared at him wild-eyed, clutching the clothes to her chest protectively. Surely he didn't expect her to bathe with her privacy ensured only by that flimsy screen?

He had turned away as if he had no doubt of her obeying his injunctions, but as she stood hesitating, he barked impatiently, "Get moving!"

She found herself moving automatically toward the screened enclosure. Once behind the barricade, she found she had more privacy than she had thought. Well, she must bathe off all this mud. She could hurry and be in and out of that sinfully luxurious tub in mere minutes. She sprinkled lavender bubble bath lavishly from a crystal container that she found near the faucets. She ripped off the muddy shorts, top, and the bra and panties beneath, and stepped into the sunken bath with a feeling of utmost luxury.

She quickly scrubbed away the mud and grass stains. Then she rested her head on the ledge at the far end of the enormous tub, stretching full length, and letting the warm silky water flow over her. She closed her eyes and it seemed that the action tuned her other senses to a keener intensity. She was conscious of the sound of running water, and the movements of Donovan as he built the fire in the fireplace across the room. There was the scent of the bubble bath, and the pungent odor of burning pine cones. How deliciously sensual and relaxing it all was, she thought drowsily . . . so relaxing.

"Brenna!"

She opened her heavy lids to stare into blue eyes that were deep and still as mountain pools. Donovan's eyes.

"Hello," she said drowsily. Somehow it seemed supremely natural to open her eyes and have Donovan there, looking at her with that quiet intensity. He was no more than a breath away, sitting on the edge of the tub and leaning close to cup her head in his hands, as he murmured huskily.

"Hello, sweetheart." His lips touched hers in a kiss as gentle as the drift of apple blossoms and sweet as honey. When his lips moved away reluctantly, she gave a little sigh of disappointment, and tilted her head in a little searching movement of frustration.

"You left the bath water running," he said hoarsely. "I called, but you didn't answer." Then his lips were there again, offering quick tender kisses to her yearning lips, her cheeks, the lobes of her ears. She turned her face up to his like a flower to the sun, her expression blindly sensual. He caught his breath raggedly, his eyes darkening with passion and his mouth covered hers, no longer gentle but burning with hunger. A demand that she met with a matching appetite. Her lips parted and his tongue stroked hers in a sensual frenzy, as he groaned low in his throat. Her hands reached up and curved around his neck to bring him closer, her fingers playing in the thick crispness of the hair at the nape of his neck, before running exploringly over the brawny muscles of his back and shoulders. "You're still wet," she whispered vaguely. Breathing heavily, he wrenched his mouth away to bury his face in her throat. She could feel the rapid tattoo of the pulse in his temple. Or was it her own feverish heartbeat, she wondered. He gave a low chuckle, "I'm about to get a lot wetter," he said huskily. "Help me with my shirt, love." He drew back and pulled his shirt from the waistband of his slacks, and then was still. "Help me," he said urgently. "I want your hands on me."

She wanted them on him, too. She obeyed the irresistible urge to touch the spring mahogany hair on his muscular chest, and then growing bolder, ran her hands up his shoulders in a slow, explorative caress. He tensed, and a shudder shook his body. He caught and held both of her hands to his chest for a brief moment before he released them with a rueful sigh. "Perhaps I'd better not have your help after all, love. I'm about to go up like all the fireworks on the Fourth of July." He stripped off the shirt, and threw it to one side, his hands swiftly going to his belt.

It was then that Brenna began to feel the first stirrings of alarm. She suddenly became conscious of the distinctly irregular situation she had become involved in. With scarlet cheeks, she looked down at herself and noticed with relief that the great quantities of bubbles cloaked everything but her shoulders in a snowy mountain of froth.

"Wait," she said shakily, her eyes on the belt Donovan had removed and was about to toss after the shirt. "What are you doing?"

Donovan's quick appraisal took in her pink cheeks and her air of distress. He moved with lightning swiftness to reassure her in a way that had her breath coming in quick gasps, and a melting ache beginning in her loins. When he finally let her go, she was clinging helplessly to him, and barely heard him when he answered between quick, hot kisses, "I want to touch you. I want to touch every inch of you. I want your hands on my body. Don't fight me, sweetheart. I won't do anything you don't want me to. I'll stop the minute you say the word."

This was poor comfort, she thought in confusion, when she wasn't at all sure she would want to say that word when the time came. At the moment she wanted nothing less than he did, and when he broke away to remove the rest of his clothing, she found she didn't even have the modesty to close her eyes. She watched with frank enjoyment as he quickly stripped, then joined her in the bath. How tough and virile he was, she thought dreamily. Those massive shoulders had an almost bull-like strength in comparison to the slim hips and strong muscular legs. "Enjoying yourself?" he asked with a grin. She nodded and smiled shyly.

As he lowered himself into the water beside her, he said, chuckling, "I feel cheated." He touched the foamy covering with one finger. "You wouldn't care to stand up and take a bow, would you?"

She shook her head with a bright blush, and he sighed. "I didn't think so. Well, as I am to be deprived of one sensual pleasure, I'll just have to make do with the others." He stretched out beside her, their bodies facing each other but not touching. "Now let me see," he said thoughtfully. "First, there's scent."

He took a strand of her hair in one hand, raised it to his nose and sniffed delicately. "You smell of fresh rainwater and the sea." He rubbed his nose against the satin skin of her temple. "Lavender," he announced hoarsely. "And woman." He drew a deep breath and murmured, "You also have a fragrance that's just you, Brenna." He closed his eyes, and said carefully, "I missed you during these past few weeks. I've been sheer hell to work with, and I didn't even know what was wrong with me. I'd never missed anyone before." He opened his eyes, and the intensity of his gaze came as a fresh shock. "I'm never going away without you again."

She knew a moment of panic at the implacable sureness of the statement. Suddenly she felt as if she were caught, caged by the sure determination of this man, who held her transfixed without even touching her.

He must have seen the flash of fear in her eyes because his intensity was instantly masked and he smiled gently. "Where were we?" he said lightly. "Oh, yes, I was about to go on to taste." His mouth touched hers gently, his tongue probing her mouth in a long dizzying exploration that left her shuddering with desire. "Honey and a dash of spice." Donovan, too, was shaking, and she could see that the muscles of his body were taut with tension. "Though your voice is music to my ears, I think we'll skip sound," he said with an effort. "I'd much prefer you silent when we go on to the next and most important step. I've got to touch you, love."

With a boldness that caused her to flinch away, she felt his hand first cradle her waist beneath the water, then draw her slowly into his arms, branding her soft nude body with his iron-hard frame.

"No," she whispered weakly, even as she felt herself melt against him, the tips of her nipples hard and sensitive as they were pressed against the rough hair of his chest. The erotic contact was sending burning messages to every nerve in her body, bidding her to respond in the ancient, primitive way of woman.

"Yes," he groaned, as his mouth took hers in savage hunger. "God! I want you. Let me love you, sweetheart."

His hands were everywhere. Stroking, probing, pressing the secret silky curves, lifting and cupping her swollen breasts to his eager mouth. She made a sound, part gasp, part moan as he nibbled and sucked at the rosy tips. He raised his head, his eyes dark and glazed. "Do you like that, love? I'll remember."

He rolled her over with one swift movement, so that he was on his back entirely supporting her slight weight, one muscular leg parting her thighs, his hands still cupping her breasts lovingly. She was now intimately conscious of his shocking arousal, as his lower body began a rhythmic thrusting motion.

She was shaking and trembling like a leaf, as he played upon her body as a master musician would on his beloved instrument. Every nerve was exquisitely sensitized to the touch of his body, and she knew that she was wildly desperate for the completion he could give her.

"I'm going to take you now, love." He breathed against her breast. "Tell me you want me to take you!"

The passionate injunction sent a spiraling shock through her, that did much to revive the thinking process which had been suspended at the command of her aching body. She knew he would keep his word and let her go, if she insisted. But, God, how could she insist, when he had tuned her body to this feverish pitch of need? Yet she knew she must refuse him, if she was to salvage any portion of her independence. Donovan was still almost a stranger to her. He had never mentioned love, only desire, and even if she did feel the same desire, it was still not enough.

"Brenna!" Donovan's voice was roughly impatient, as he waited for the acquiescence that he fully expected.

It was the hardest thing she ever did to look into Donovan's eyes and say huskily, "Let me go, Michael."

His face echoed his shocked disbelief, and his hands tightened on her possessively. Then his eyes flamed with anger. "You don't mean that," he said roughly. "You want it as much as I do."

She shook her head stubbornly. "I want you to let me go," she said shakily. "I want you to keep your promise, Michael Donovan."

His eyes narrowed and there was a ruthless curve to his mouth as he said coolly, "You know I could force you to say yes."

She said honestly, "Yes, you probably could. I seem to have little resistance where you're concerned." She looked fearlessly into his eyes. "But I don't think you will.

You value your integrity, and that wouldn't really be keeping your word, would it?"

There was a flash of anger in the hot blue eyes as he pushed her away with a violent shove.

"Damn you!" he said harshly. With rapid, jerky movements, he was out of the tub, wrapping one of the towels around his waist. As he looked down at her, there was a fierce savagery about his tautly held body that caused her to shrink back against the side of the tub.

"Get out of there and get dressed. I'll give you exactly three minutes!"

He strode from the enclosure, pushing aside the screen with a violence that threatened to topple it. She heard the soft thud of his bare feet on the spiral staircase, before she scrambled out of the tub and dried hurriedly. He hadn't said what would happen in three minutes, but if his expression was any harbinger, she didn't want to find out. She grabbed frantically at the clothes on the floor at the edge of the tub and donned a pair of green swimming trunks that came almost to her knees and a white short-sleeved shirt that was equally voluminous. Looking down at herself ruefully, she knew she looked a complete sketch. If any outfit was designed to turn a man off, this one was. She refused to ask herself why she felt a niggling sense of dissatisfaction with her appearance. After all, that was what she wanted, wasn't it? Even a Marilyn Monroe would have been safe in a costume like this.

She stepped hesitantly from behind the screen just as Donovan came down the stairs. Dressed in faded jeans and a pale blue workman's shirt he looked devastatingly virile and attractive. He finished rolling up the sleeves as he came toward her. His face was expressionless, but there was an undeniable tenseness about him that made her look away involuntarily. A caustic smile curving his mouth, he walked past her to the bar and poured himself a drink.

"You'll find a comb and brush upstairs on the bedside table," he said coolly. "I'll put the steaks on."

Her eyes widened. "We aren't leaving?"

"It's still raining," he pointed out. "You'd be drenched again before we got halfway to the 'copter."

"I wouldn't mind," she said hesitantly.

"Well, I would," he said decisively. "We have two more days of shooting before the picture is finished. I can't afford to have you ill." He took a long swallow of his drink.

"I see," she said shakily, her doe eyes wide with pain.

"Damn!" Donovan slammed his glass down on the bar. "What do you expect of me, Brenna? You tease me until I'm almost insane with wanting you, then turn me off cool as a cucumber. And when I display a little bad temper, you look at me as if I'd slapped you!"

"I never meant to tease you," she whispered huskily, tears brimming.

"No, I don't think you did," he said moodily. "That's why we're having this discussion down here, instead of upstairs on that king-sized bed." He ran a hand through his hair. "I can't figure you out."

She shrugged wearily. "I'm not very complicated, Michael."

"The hell you're not," he said bluntly. "You want me, I know you do. Yet you're behaving like a frightened virgin instead of the experienced woman you are. I don't know what kind of bastard it was who messed you up like this, but if I ever meet this ex-lover of yours, I'll probably kill him."

She almost smiled at how close he had come to the truth. She was indeed a frightened virgin. But she wasn't frightened of sex, as he surmised. She would have welcomed her first experience with delight, if she could have been assured that the joy would not turn to ashes after the first flames faded.

Donovan picked up his drink and drained it. He looked directly into her eyes, and said quietly, "Someday you're going to belong to me in all the ways there are, Brenna, and you're going to enjoy it completely!" He put the glass down on the bar and looked down at it thoughtfully. "I've been very patient for me, but I've reached the end of the road." He looked up, and said coolly, "What I'm saying is, that after I take you home today, the gloves are off."

She smiled uncertainly. "You pounce!" she said jokingly.

"I pounce," he affirmed softly. He turned away, his long strides carrying him to the kitchen. "As for now, you can enjoy your temporary reprieve. The steaks should be done in about ten minutes."

She was too tense to obey this injunction in the hours that followed. Donovan was the perfect host. He conducted an urbane and noncommital conversation that was designed to put her at ease, but only succeeded in increasing her nervousness. Despite his self-control, there was an undercurrent of restrained violence about him that was reminiscent of the rumble that preceded the eruption of a volcano.

After they had eaten the really excellent steak and salad Donovan had prepared, they had coffee before the fire. Even the glowing intimacy induced by these cozy surroundings brought no change in Donovan's demeanor, and Brenna began to relax. She should have known that Donovan always meant exactly what he said. She was safe for today.

The rain stopped late in the afternoon, and Donovan made immediate preparations to leave, indicating that he was just as eager as she to end this strained situation.

They arrived back at the residence hall well before sunset. As Donovan drew the Mercedes to a halt at the front entrance, she turned to face him, her hand on the door handle. "You don't have to come with me," she said quickly. "I have to stop at reception to make sure Randy's all right."

His mouth tightened. "I'll come with you," he said decisively. "I promised to deliver you back to the cottage, and I'm going to do just that," he added bitterly. "We both know how I value my promises."

As she got out of the car, she realized what a ludicrous sight she must present in Donovan's outsized clothes, her long hair in two thick braids down her back. She must look about ten years old, she thought wryly.

There was no censure on the receptionist's face, as they entered the lobby. Paula Drummond's manner was almost obsequiously servile, when she noticed Donovan following closely behind Brenna.

When Brenna asked if there had been any messages from Doris Charles, the girl checked her box, and then said brightly, "She left word that they will be at the pool till seven. The shower this afternoon prevented Randy from having his afternoon swim, so she brought him down about half an hour ago."

Brenna nodded. "Then I'll go down to the cottage and change," she said. "Will you tell Doris that I'll be up to see Randy before he goes to bed?"

Paula nodded, still shooting curious glances at Donovan's expressionless face. "I sure will," she said cheerfully. "Oh! I almost forgot. There was a message for you." She shuffled the cards efficiently. "Mr. Paul Chadeaux," she announced. "He phoned about ten this morning and then again about an hour ago. The last time he called he left a message." She turned the card over. "He wants to see you, and he will call on you about eight tonight."

Brenna turned away from the desk, her face suddenly white. She moved numbly, her limbs working automatically to carry her out the far door and down the path to the cottage. She was hardly conscious of Donovan following her till she was almost halfway to the cottage. Then he grasped her elbow with an iron hand.

"Who is Paul Chadeaux?" Donovan asked harshly.

Who was Paul Chadeaux? What should she answer, she thought almost hysterically. The man who was responsible for her sister's death. The father of Janine's baby. The devil incarnate. My God, what did he want with her? She hadn't even seen him for almost three years, and he'd never even seemed to notice Janine's kid sister. The answer was heartstoppingly obvious: Randy.

Donovan's hand tightened, and he spun her around to face him. "Answer me, Brenna," Donovan ordered fiercely. "Who is this Chadeaux?" His face was set, his blue eyes narrowed suspiciously. "If he's some boyfriend who has followed you from Los Angeles, you can just get rid of him. I won't have you seeing any other man. Do you hear me?"

She broke away from him, hardly knowing what she was doing, her stride automatically lengthening as she neared the cottage. "I'll have to see him," she murmured. She had to be alone, she thought desperately. She had to think what to do. She had to be prepared when she saw Chadeaux again. Oh, God! It was almost seven!

She could vaguely feel the anger emanating from Donovan, as he silently escorted her to the cottage and waited while she unlocked the door.

"I'm not leaving until you tell me who this man is, Brenna," he said tightly. "He must be damned important to upset you like this."

"You have to go," she said distractedly. She knew she couldn't cope with a jealous Michael Donovan right now.

"Who is he, Brenna?" Donovan asked inexorably.

"He's Randy's father," Brenna answered desperately. "Now will you leave?"

Donovan muttered a curse beneath his breath, before he said harshly, "You don't have to see the bastard. I'll notify security that he's not to get within a mile of you."

"No!" Brenna said sharply. "Don't do that. I have to see what he wants."

"You want to see him?" Donovan's voice had a dangerous softness.

"I *have* to see him," Brenna said wearily. "Now will you please go, Michael?"

There was a muttered imprecation, and

then Donovan turned on his heel and strode angrily away.

SEVEN

Brenna entered the cottage and closed the door with a sigh of relief. Until this minute, she hadn't been sure that Donovan would really leave. She felt a trace of surprise that he had left without an argument, and she knew she had not seen the last of him this evening. But he was at least giving her the breathing space she needed badly. There was so little time before she had to meet Chadeaux.

Why did he want to see her after all this time, she wondered frantically. In the first wild bitterness after Janine's tragic death, Brenna had wanted to confront Chadeaux with his guilt, but she had refrained for Janine's sake. Janine had been so fanatically opposed to Randy having anything to do with his father, that Brenna had felt any contact with Chadeaux would be a betrayal of trust.

She cynically discarded the idea that

Chadeaux may have discovered paternal feelings at this late date. He had been too eager in his insistence that Janine have an abortion, and too brutal in his rejection of both her and the baby, when he had thought that there might be repercussions from their affair.

Her mind raced wildly in circles, trying to find an answer and finally giving up in despair. She would have to wait for the meeting with Chadeaux. But whatever he wanted, he would not find her as easy to deal with as Janine, she resolved with unaccustomed hardness.

Brenna marched decisively into the bedroom, and threw open the closet door. The first order of business was to convince Chadeaux that he was not dealing with a naïve youngster but a sophisticated adult.

Forty-five minutes later she looked with approval at the reflection in the mirror. The pink, sleeveless *cheongsam* with its high mandarin collar and the stylish slits on each side of the skirt gave her just the air of worldliness she desired. She had brushed out the childish braids and piled her hair on top of her head, leaving several wispy strands to curl around her face alluringly, and the dashing gold earrings were definitely not for the nursery set. She had used more

165

makeup than usual, and her doe eyes appeared enormous in the perfect oval of her face. She slipped on bone high-heeled sandals, with a hurried look at the clock on the bedside table. It was almost eight, she noticed with panic. Not that time had ever meant anything to Paul Chadeaux. One of the things that had most annoyed her about Chadeaux, when he was dating her sister, was his constant and discourteous tardiness. He clearly had not reformed in that respect, for it was almost eight-fifteen before there was a knock at the door.

When Brenna opened the door, she experienced a small shock. Her hatred and disgust for Paul Chadeaux were such that she had expected the marks of guilt and weakness to be reflected on his face. Instead, he looked the same as on that first day Janine had introduced her to him. The same carefully styled blond hair and rather expressionless gray eyes, the same aristocratic features and full sensual lips curved now in a mocking smile. He had always dressed rather formally, and that, too, had not changed. The steel gray business suit was faultlessly tailored to flatter his tall, lean frame.

His gray eyes roved over her with insulting intimacy. "Well, well," he drawled softly.

"Little sister has grown up, and very nicely, too. I'd hardly recognize you as the skinny kid that used to stare at me so antagonistically with those big brown eyes."

Her mouth twisted bitterly. "You'll find I'm still antagonistic, Paul," she said coolly. "And I hardly think you're here to reminisce about old times. Perhaps you'd better come in." She closed the door, and preceded him into the living room. She was amazed that she could present such a composed facade, when inwardly she was shaking with fear and revulsion. She was a better actress than she thought.

Chadeaux gave a low whistle, as he looked around appreciatively at the luxurious appointments of the cottage. "Very nice," he said. "You're obviously doing very well for yourself. So little Brenna is going to be a big movie star."

"Nonsense!" she said sharply. "I have a small supporting role in my first film. How did you know where to find me, Paul?"

He shrugged. "Your landlady was very cooperative when I told her the kid was mine," he said casually. "She seemed to think you were his mother. Maybe she thought I was going to make an honest woman of you at last." He seemed to find the idea very amusing, and Brenna had to clench her fists to

167

keep from slapping the smug smile off his face.

"Why did you want to see me?" she asked bluntly.

"You're not being very hospitable," he complained mockingly. "Aren't you going to offer me a drink?"

She drew an impatient breath, and said quickly, "No, I'm not going to offer you a drink. I don't want you here. Please state your business and get out."

His mouth twisted, and his gray eyes took on an ugly glint. "You always were an uppity bitch," he said sneeringly. "You never did like me, did you, little sister?"

"No, I never did," she said flatly. "I like you even less now. Why are you here?"

He crossed the room and seated himself in the lavender wing chair without asking permission. "I want the kid," he said mockingly. "I've decided it's time I heard the patter of little feet around my lonely bachelor pad."

She stared at him incredulously. "You can't be serious," she said scornfully.

"Oh, but I am," he said, lazily stretching his legs out before him. "I've gone to a great deal of time and trouble to track the kid down. Don't make the mistake of thinking I'm not totally sincere in my devotion."

He took a gold cigarette case out of his jacket pocket, selected a cigarette and lit it leisurely. "I actually started out looking for Janine. Then I found out that she was dead, and that you had the child. Then I had to trace your whereabouts," he said complainingly. "It's all been a complete bore."

"How sorry we are to inconvenience you," Brenna said ironically.

"I should think you would be," he said pettishly, ignoring her sarcasm. "After all, I am willing to take the kid off your hands."

"The 'kid's' name is Randy," she said, between clenched teeth.

"I know. I know," Chadeaux said impatiently. "Your landlady told me that. Run along and get him, will you? I want to get the night coach back to San Francisco."

Brenna's eyes narrowed suspiciously. "San Francisco? I thought you lived in Los Angeles."

He shrugged, his eyes sliding away from hers. "I thought I'd drop Randy off at the Chadeaux vineyards. He'll be better off with my family."

"You couldn't care less about Randy," Brenna charged bitterly. "Why do you really want him, Paul?"

An unpleasant smile touched his full lips. "I don't really have to answer to you," he

169

said arrogantly. "But I will. Why not?"

He drew on his cigarette lazily. "My grandmother is all hung up on this dynasty thing. She's been nagging me for years to marry and settle down. They want a fitting heir for the Chadeaux Wineries. One they can mold into the good little boy I never was," he said sneeringly. "The old lady has already told me that unless I provide her with an heir, she'll stop my allowance and cut me out of her will."

"Don't you think she'll object to an illegitimate child?" Brenna said caustically. "I seem to remember that you told my sister that you'd refuse to acknowledge the baby if Janine went to your family."

"Situations change," he said with satisfaction. "The old lady is getting desperate. She'll welcome the kid with open arms. She's even promised to settle up my gambling debts."

"Providing you give her Randy," Brenna said grimly, her face mirroring her rage and disgust.

Her contempt pierced even Chadeaux's thick ego. "Get the kid!" he ordered angrily.

"Go to hell!" Brenna said deliberately. "Randy is mine now, and I'm not giving him up."

Chadeaux's face flushed with anger. "Listen, bitch," he said coldly. "I'm the kid's father. You're just his aunt. I have a right to him."

"You forfeited any rights you had before he was born," Brenna said. "I wouldn't turn a stray dog over to you, much less a small child."

"You may not have a choice. The Chadeaux family have very important connections in California. I think any court in the state will lean toward the natural father over the claim of some little actress."

She smiled sweetly. "But then it's up to you to prove that you're the natural father, isn't it? I think you'll find that a little difficult."

His eyes narrowed warily. "What the hell do you mean? Janine told me I was the father."

"And you rejected her," Brenna said bitterly, her mouth curling. "Is it any wonder that Janine refused to name the father on Randy's birth certificate?"

He shrugged. "I can get around that. There are plenty of witnesses that knew Janine and I were having an affair at the time. I'm the only logical candidate."

Brenna smiled triumphantly. "You would be, if it was Janine Sloan that gave birth to Randy," she said softly. "But according to the birth certificate, she didn't. Brenna Sloan did."

Chadeaux's mouth gaped open. "You're lying," he accused angrily. "That's totally absurd. Why would Janine do a crazy thing like that."

"Perhaps in the end she was a little crazy," Brenna said, her eyes clouded with pain. "Crazy with fear and rejection and loneliness. Crazy to protect the one human being that was to be hers alone. I thought it was insane, too, but now I wonder if she somehow knew that Randy would need to be protected from you."

Chadeaux jumped to his feet, his fists clenched. "You won't get away with this," he snapped. "I need that kid, and I'll find a way of getting him. You're just making it a little more difficult. I'll hire detectives who will punch a million holes in your story. They'll turn up a dozen witnesses who will swear you're not Randy's mother."

Brenna felt a chill at the threat, but she couldn't let him know he'd frightened her. "It will take a long time to do that," she said coolly. "Do you really have that much time? I believe you mentioned something about gambling debts?"

There was a speculative look in the shallow gray eyes as he looked her over critically. "We might come to an agreement," he said slowly. "You want the kid. I need the money. Grandmother wants me settled with a wife and family. What do you say we make everybody happy? Why don't we fly to Vegas and get married?"

Brenna could feel the blood drain from her face in shock. "You must be mad," she whispered. "I can't stand the sight of you."

"I'm not overly fond of you, either," Paul said caustically. "You're too independent. I was going to make the offer to Janine, when I found her. She was much more my type."

Suddenly Brenna couldn't stand any more. She felt sick at the sight of him.

"Get out!" she said harshly. "I don't ever want to see you again."

"Well, that's too bad," he said nastily. "Because you're going to see a hell of a lot of me in the next few months. In court and out, little sister!"

"If you don't leave, I'll call security to force you to go," Brenna said tensely.

"Oh, I'm leaving," Chadeaux said, as he bent to crush out his cigarette in the crystal ashtray on the table. "But don't think I won't be back." He strolled casually over to the door, and turned to look at her as he opened it.

There was such a malevolent viciousness

in his expression that she caught her breath in fear. "Good-bye, little sister! See you soon."

As the door closed she flew over to it and locked it hurriedly, as if to lock out the threat that had been evident in Chadeaux's last statement. He meant it. Chadeaux would stop at nothing to get Randy, now that he saw an advantage in it. There was no way she could let the little boy fall into those carelessly cruel hands, she thought frantically. She walked into the living room, pacing agitatedly back and forth, trying to see some solution to the problem. She hadn't a doubt that given time, Chadeaux could produce the witnesses he needed to press his claim. Janine's ploy had been flimsy at best. How could Brenna stop him if he actually took her to court? His arguments had merit. The Chadeaux family had great wealth and power. How could she possibly fight them if it came to a custody battle? She froze, as an even worse thought came to her. What if Chadeaux got an injunction giving him temporary custody of Randy pending the outcome of the trial?

She whirled, and ran into the bedroom. She took two suitcases out of the closet and threw them on the bed before picking up the telephone extension and dialing reception. "Paula, this is Brenna Sloan. I've got to leave at once for Los Angeles. An emergency. Will you contact Doris and have her pack for Randy, and have him ready to leave in twenty minutes? And I'll need Johnny to drive me to Portland to get a flight." Paula Drummond answered with her usual bright efficiency, expressing polite concern before she hung up.

Brenna started to fill the open suitcase, tossing in the clothes with no regard to neatness or order. She was well aware it was panic that spurred her to this rash decision, but what else could she do? Her only chance of keeping Randy from Chadeaux was to disappear with Randy and hide. It was only money that motivated Chadeaux's desire for Randy. If she could remain undercover long enough, Chadeaux would have to find another solution to his money problems. Then, perhaps, he would consider the child the burden and annoyance he had previously.

She had filled one suitcase and was halfway through with the second, when there was a knock on the front door. That would be Johnny. She started to call out for him to come in, when she realized that she had locked the door. "Just a minute, Johnny."

She hurriedly crossed to the door to let him in.

Michael Donovan brushed her aside and strode into the cottage. He crossed to the open bedroom door, and, with a raking glance, took in the open suitcases and the hurried preparations for departure. He turned slowly, and Brenna flinched at his furious expression and blazing eyes. In their short acquaintance she had seen him angry many times, but never like this. He looked like a dangerous animal ready to spring.

"Johnny won't be coming," he said softly. "I told Paula I would attend to everything."

Brenna bit her lip to keep it from trembling. "Does Paula always act as a spy for you?" she asked shakily. The sight of him had been a shock that threatened to vanquish the little control she still had over her emotions.

"Not always," Donovan said harshly. "Let's just say, she knew I'd be interested in your little emergency!" His leashed anger broke through its bonds. "My God! That bastard only had to get you alone for an hour, to make you go running back to him like a bitch in heat. Don't you have any pride or self-respect? The son of a bitch got you pregnant and then deserted you!"

She was stunned. He actually thought she

was running to Chadeaux instead of away from him. The ridiculousness of the surmise seemed wildly funny in her desperate state, and she laughed hysterically.

It was a mistake. In two strides he had reached her, his hands gripping her shoulders brutally as he shook her. "Shut up, damn you!" he rasped, his eyes like hot coals in his white face. "Do you think I'm just going to let you walk away from me? You're not going to him. I'll stop you any way I can." His eyes were tormented as they ran over her contemptuously. "Look at you. You couldn't wait to get rid of me, so that you could dress up for him. Did it work? Did he think you were even more beautiful than he remembered? Is that why he asked you to come back to him?"

"No! no! You've got it all wrong. I'd never do that. I couldn't." Tears were running down her cheeks as the last of her fragile control vanished. "I hate him," she said brokenly. Suddenly she collapsed against him, clinging to his rock-like strength with desperation, her body wracked with sobs.

Donovan was frozen with surprise for a long moment, and then his arms went slowly around her to hold her securely. "Then why are you going back to him?" he asked bluntly. "Does he have some kind of hold on you? For God's sake, tell me what's wrong, Brenna."

"He wants Randy," she said baldly. "He's going to take Randy away from me." She stepped back reluctantly from that magically warming embrace, and immediately felt alone and vulnerable again. "I was trying to run away from him," she said wearily.

"You were also running away from me," Donovan said coolly. "And any chance you might have for a career. Do you think any film-maker in the business would take a chance on you again, once it got around that you'd run out before the picture was finished?"

"No, I guess I didn't think at all," Brenna admitted huskily. "But I still would have done the same thing if I had. I can't let Paul Chadeaux get his hands on Randy." She wiped her eyes childishly with the back of her hand.

"No one is going to take your child away from you," Donovan said with conviction. "I won't let them. If you had come to me instead of flying into a panic, I'd have told you that."

She shook her head ruefully at the sheer royal arrogance of the man. It would not happen, because Donovan did not will it so. Long live Michael Donovan. In spite of herself, she couldn't help being a little re-assured by his boundless confidence. Aside from their burgeoning personal relationship, Donovan had a business interest in seeing that Brenna Sloan completed his picture on schedule. He would bend the same ruthless energy to her problem as to any other obstacle that got in his way.

She opened her lips to confess that Randy was not her child but Janine's. She knew he was entitled to know everything, if she was going to solicit his help. Under the circumstances, Janine would surely forgive her for breaking her promise. Suddenly Brenna was beset by doubts. Would Donovan be as eager to help her if he knew the child wasn't hers? He had no affection for Randy. Wouldn't he, like everyone else, think that she should turn Randy over to his natural father? She couldn't take the chance. Randy was too important to her.

Donovan strolled over to the bar and made himself a drink. Pouring her a small whiskey, he returned to hand it to her.

She accepted it, a small smile curving her lips. "This seems to be your day for plying me with liquor," she said.

"You need it," he said curtly. "Now suppose you tell me why you think Chadeaux has a chance of gaining custody of Randy.

Didn't you say the father wasn't named on the birth certificate?"

Not looking at him, Brenna briefly related Chadeaux's threats. She purposely did not mention Janine, leaving Donovan to assume that it was Chadeaux's intention to hire detectives to find witnesses to their affair that had so terrified her.

"That's all?" Donovan asked, his eyes narrowed on her flushed face. "You're sure he wasn't trying to blackmail you? He didn't offer to leave Randy with you for a consideration?"

Brenna shook her head, relieved that he had mistaken her guilt for distress. She made a face. "He made an offer," she admitted dryly. "But I couldn't take marriage with Paul Chadeaux even for Randy."

Donovan looked at his drink. "Marriage," he said thoughtfully. "The bastard must know you very well. In time, when you'd gotten desperate enough, you might have given in to even that. It's obvious you'd do anything for the child." He took a long swallow of his drink. "It makes you very vulnerable, Brenna. I can see that I'm going to have to build a fence around you to keep out the predators."

"A fence?" Brenna asked blankly.

"I'm going to marry you myself," Donovan said coolly.

She felt her heart lurch, and the blood rush dizzily to her head. "That's not very funny," she said breathlessly, moistening her lips.

"It wasn't intended to be," Donovan said calmly. "I've just offered you a solution to your problem. Marriage to me would safeguard your claim to Randy, and protect you from any further harassment from Chadeaux. I know how to take care of my own."

"He could still locate those witnesses and push his claim to Randy."

His eyes were totally ruthless. "Not if I claim that I'm Randy's father. I don't relish the idea of casting myself as a seducer of a teenage Lolita, but I imagine my word would be taken over Chadeaux's. I pour a lot of money into the state's economy, and I have a few friends in high places."

Brenna's eyes were wide with shock. "No one would believe you," she said. "I didn't even know you three years ago."

Donovan shrugged. "Who's to know that?" he asked sardonically. "For every witness that Chadeaux produces to testify that you were his mistress, I'll have two to swear you were mine. In case you haven't heard, money talks!"

"You'd pay someone to perjure them-selves?" Brenna asked, aghast.

"If necessary," Donovan said bluntly. "Would you rather lose Randy? There are no guarantees that you'll get justice just because you're right. Sometimes justice has to be manipulated." He smiled tightly. "However, it may not come to that. Your ex-lover seems to be a little on the shady side. I may be able to put the screws on him in some other way. I'll get my lawyers on it tomorrow." He drained his glass, and set it down on the coffee table. "It would be best if we were married immediately," he said simply. "Shall we say, three days? That will take care of the waiting period, and give you a chance to finish the picture. I'll send the company doctor by the set tomorrow to take care of the blood test."

"Wait!" Brenna protested, holding up her hand distractedly. "I've got to think. It's all going too fast." Donovan was proceeding with his usual steamroller tactics, and she felt she would be swept away in the wake of his single-minded drive like a leaf in a storm if she didn't slow him down.

"What's to think about?" Donovan asked impatiently. "You get your son, your career, and a wealthy husband. What more could you want?"

The bitter cynicism in his face hurt her in some mysterious fashion. "Why are you doing this?" she asked bewilderedly. "Yes, I'm getting all that, but what are you getting out of this marriage?"

The blue eyes were suddenly impenetrable as Donovan considered her question. "What am I getting?" His mouth twisted cynically. "I'm getting Brenna Sloan in my bed until I tire of her. I get a chance to work off this obsession I have for you. Closeness has been known to kill stone dead more than one great passion. Maybe I'll get lucky."

"You expect me to . . ." Brenna blushed, and then was furious with herself when Donovan raised an eyebrow mockingly.

"You're damn right I do," he said bluntly. "This isn't some storybook. This is real life, Brenna. There's always a price tag on everything. Sometimes it's hidden, but the price is there. In this case, I don't think you'll find it hard to pay."

Brenna shivered. "You make it sound so . . . business-like," she said unhappily.

"I think I can promise you it won't be at all business-like once we're in bed," he said dryly. "We really turn each other on, remember? I told you once I don't play games. I like all the cards on the table. For saving your son for you, all I want is your word that you won't leave me until I tell you to go."

Brenna's mouth twisted wryly. "Yet you retain the right to toss me aside whenever you get bored with me," she said sadly. "Jake said you always had an escape clause written into every contract."

There was a flicker of emotion deep in Donovan's eyes before he looked away. "That's right, I do," he said coolly. "Do I have your promise?"

Brenna's throat was tight and aching as she looked at Donovan's hard, expressionless face. She had a fleeting memory of another Donovan walking with her hand in hand through the woods. Why did it hurt so much to realize she might never reach further than the physical with this man?

"Yes, you have my promise," she said wearily.

"Good," Donovan said briskly, as if he had never expected anything else. He dropped a light kiss on her forehead as if she were a small child. "You'd better get to bed. You're exhausted. I'll see you tomorrow."

Her face must have reflected her surprise, for a sardonic smile twisted Donovan's mouth. "You expected me to drag you off to bed once I had your word? You must have had some poor lovers, Brenna. Now that I

have a commitment from you, I can wait."
He grimaced. "Not long, but I can wait."
She was staring after him, still speechless,
when the door closed behind him.

EIGHT

Brenna sipped her champagne, gazing over the crowded living room with a curious feeling of remoteness. It was almost as if she were a guest and not the central figure at this wedding reception. There was no possibility of her occupying center stage with Michael Donovan in the same scene, she thought wryly. Even the glamour surrounding the bride was eclipsed by a groom with Donovan's dynamic charisma.

Not that she had been neglected. On the contrary, she had been fussed over and toadied to, to such an extent that she was forced to move to this quiet corner to escape. She had no illusions that it was her own charm that had instigated such an effusive display. Two hours ago the little nobody actress had become Mrs. Michael Donovan, and so must be cultivated. She had the ear of the throne.

"A bride for such a short time and left all

alone? Michael isn't usually so careless with his possessions." Jake Dominic's mocking voice made her look up quickly. Devastatingly attractive, as usual, in conventional black evening clothes, he was a welcome sight to Brenna, after putting up with the fawning sycophants all evening.

"He appears to be busy," Brenna said calmly, her eyes searching out Donovan's red head in a far corner of the room, as he bent to listen attentively to a distinguished gray-haired man.

"Judge Simon Arthington, State Supreme Court Judge," Jake said thoughtfully. "And before that, I saw him with Senator Atkins. Unusual company to cultivate on one's wedding day, wouldn't you say?"

"Perhaps he's just being a good host," Brenna said evasively. "They are friends of his, aren't they?"

"Oh, they're friends of his," Jake said cynically. "Michael is a very generous contributor to their campaign funds. They're very fond of him." He looked around the room distastefully. "I see several other 'friends' of Michael's here." He shrugged, and turned to smile charmingly at her. "Have I told you how lovely you are tonight? You're something out of Tolstoy."

She smiled back at him, wrinkling her

nose saucily. "I should be. I was too busy slaving for you to go shopping, so Michael had wardrobe run me up this little number. I have an idea it was originally meant for a remake of *War and Peace*."

All joking aside, she really loved the gown. It was an exquisitely simple garment in lemon yellow, embroidered with white daisies. The empire cut and low round neck merely hinted gracefully at the smallness of her waist and hips, but boldly accented the swell of her breasts. She wore no jewelry and only a garland of daisies on her head. Her hair had been brushed to a sensuous silken sheen and allowed to fall almost to her waist, to complement the romantic aura of the gown.

"Oh, yes, Michael was in a great hurry for this wedding, wasn't he?" Jake asked casually. "But not too hurried to arrange this elaborate reception for you, Brenna. I suppose you're very fond of parties. Most women are."

Brenna made a face. "I hate them," she said frankly. "This kind, at least. I enjoyed the one on the set yesterday, to celebrate the end of the picture. Michael made all the arrangements for the wedding and reception."

"Curiouser and curiouser," Jake said

softly, black eyes gleaming. "I happen to know that Michael is bored to death at parties. He never attends one unless it's absolutely necessary for business reasons. Then, when he's finished, he's usually found in a corner, munching dip and glowering bad-temperedly. Yet on the most private and personal event of his life, he throws an elaborate party, invites people he couldn't care less about, except to use. And he proceeds to ignore his beautiful bride, who he's obviously crazy about, and spends his time cultivating judges and senators!" Jake's expression was as alert and watchful as a pouncing cat as he asked mildly, "You wouldn't know anything about all this, would you, Brenna?"

Brenna looked down at her champagne. "Why should I know anything?" she asked quietly. "Michael always does what he wants to do."

Jake's eyebrows rose cynically. "And if you do, you're not about to satisfy my curiosity," he said knowingly.

Brenna looked up, a smile lifting the corners of her mouth. "Exactly," she said succinctly.

He sighed. "I was afraid of that," he said. "I couldn't get anything out of Michael, either."

"Why should you bother, Jake?" Brenna asked curiously. "Michael knows what he's doing."

"None better," Jake agreed lightly. "I suppose I'm feeling a touch of unaccustomed responsibility. I've never been a best man before."

"You were very convincing," Brenna assured him solemnly. "You and Nora practically stole the show. It was nice of Nora to be my maid of honor, wasn't it?"

"She likes you," Jake said simply. "The whole crew likes you. You're a very popular person, Brenna Sloan. I even like you."

Brenna sketched a mocking curtsy, her brown eyes dancing at such a graceless compliment from a man who was reputed to have one of the smoothest lines in the world. "I am duly honored," she said demurely.

"You should be," he said dryly. "I don't think I've ever told a woman I liked her before. It may be a first for the *Guinness Book of World Records*."

Brenna let out a little bubble of laughter. Dominic cocked his head, a pleased smile on his face, "I do like that laugh of yours. Most women giggle or tinkle. You sort of gurgle like running water. You should do it more often."

"Working under you isn't a matter for laughter, Jake Dominic," Brenna said severely. "You almost killed me."

"You held up better than most actresses would." He shrugged. "You have stamina."

It was a compliment to be treasured from Jake Dominic, and Brenna began to feel as if the heartbreaking, exhausting work may have been worth it after all.

"I saw the final rushes last night," Jake said slowly. "They were good." He took a sip of his champagne. "You were damn good."

Brenna's eyes flew to his face.

He looked at her steadily, taking his time. "You were so good, that everyone in the audience is going to wonder why Dirk jilted you for Nora." He frowned teasingly. "You've endangered the credibility of my masterpiece."

"Jake, do you mean . . ." Brenna trailed off breathlessly, afraid to continue.

"I mean that you were great," he said simply. "I mean that Donovan has not only got himself a wife, he's got himself a new star."

"Jake!" Brenna exclaimed exuberantly, launching herself into his arms. Careless of their champagne glasses, and the glances of the amused guests, she hugged him ecstatically.

They were both laughing hilariously, Jake holding her around the waist with one arm, while he rescued the champagne glasses with the other, when Brenna felt a hand on her shoulder.

Donovan plucked her neatly from Jake's embrace, to rest possessively in the curve of his arm. "Mine, I believe," he said coolly to Jake. Then his eyes went to Brenna, and her smile faded as she met the dangerous glint in his. "I'm happy to see you're enjoying yourself, my dear," he said silkily. "It's the most animation I've seen you display today."

"Take it easy, Michael," Jake advised softly. "She was just happy. I told her about the rushes."

Donovan's tension relaxed fractionally, but his tone was still less than cordial when he said, "I've had enough of this charade, Brenna. It's time we left."

Dominic raised his eyebrow and gave Brenna an I-told-you-so glance. "I would slip away quietly if you want to avoid the usual embarrassing remarks and foolishness. My car is parked in front of the residence hall." He handed Donovan the keys. "I wouldn't suggest you use your Mercedes. I heard some of the stunt boys plotting to rig up yours à la James Bond."

A reluctant smile creased Donovan's face, as he shook his head ruefully. "My God! What will they be up to next? Thanks, Jake."

With Dominic urbanely covering their retreat, Donovan and Brenna quietly exited through the kitchen door, and made their way quickly up the path in the direction of the residence hall.

"I've arranged to have Randy and Doris Charles moved from their quarters to my home tomorrow," Donovan said abruptly. "I thought under the circumstances that we would dispense with the usual honeymoon nonsense and just go directly there tonight."

Brenna was aware that Donovan had his own home a short distance away from the main complex of Twin Pines, so this decision came as no surprise to her. Donovan's workload for the next few months would be staggering with both the post-production for *Forgotten Moment* and the start of the filming of *Wild Heritage* on the agenda. Brenna was surprised at the curiously defensive note in Donovan's usually urbane manner. Had he really thought that she would expect the usual romantic trappings despite the conditions of her marriage?

"Yes, of course," she said serenely. "It would be a foolish gesture when you have such a full schedule."

For some reason the sweet reasonableness of this statement seemed to only increase Donovan's irritation and a black scowl clouded his face. "How very sensible of you," he said caustically. "And how lucky I am to have such a pragmatic bride."

Pragmatic? That was hardly the correct word to describe her mood at this moment, she thought. She was married to this red-headed dynamo, who had taken charge of her life, and changed it out of all recognition. This was her wedding night. In a short time, she would give herself to him in the most intimate, physical sense. Why wasn't she frightened, she wondered. She was excited, nervous, and even shy, but not frightened.

Donovan was moodily silent on the short drive to his home, and it was only as they pulled into the curving driveway and halted before an extremely large, two-story house of mellow pink brick, that the silence was broken.

"It's perfectly lovely," Brenna said softly, gazing at the house.

It was lovely. There was an indescribable beauty about the house with it's wide bay windows and climbing ivy. It had a subtle air of welcoming warmth and permanency about it, that was at odds with the rest of the modern style architecture of Twin Pines.

Donovan smiled mockingly. "You're surprised? I thought you would be. When I had the house built, I told the architect I wanted it to look like it had been here for a hundred years and would be here for another hundred. I live a fast life that has constantly changing values. I like the idea of having some semblance of permanence to come home to.

"There are no live-in servants," he went on coolly. "I have a woman from town, a Mrs. Haskins, who comes daily and two girls who come in twice a week. Besides that there is the gardener and all-around handyman, Joe Peters. Oh, yes. I've recently hired a chauffeur for you, Bob Phillips."

She looked at him, startled. "I don't need a driver," she protested. "I wouldn't know what to do with one."

"You're a lady of substance now," he said mockingly. "You'll get used to it."

She doubted that. But looking around the foyer a few minutes later, she knew she would have no problem getting used to this aspect of Donovan's wealth. There was nothing pretentious about the decor. She had half-expected antiques after Donovan's statement in the car, but this was not the

case. The house was decorated in no particular period, and with only one general
theme: comfort. Every piece of furniture
that graced the house had the mellow patina
of expert craftsmanship, lovingly executed.

"I think coffee is in order, after all that
champagne," Donovan said briskly. "I want
to talk." He gestured to the double door in
richly glowing mahogany. "If you'd like to
go into the library and make yourself comfortable, I'll bring it through."

"Couldn't I go with you?" she asked impulsively.

He arched an eyebrow. "Why not?" he
asked with a shrug, and she followed him
down the hall to the large bright kitchen
done entirely in sunshine yellow and white.

"Sit down," he said casually, waving to the
breakfast bar with its high stools upholstered
in rich white leather. "I'll be with you in a
minute."

As Brenna perched on a high stool and
watched him as he measured coffee into the
chrome percolator, she thought what an
incongruous sight they must present in their
ultra-modern surroundings. She in her
romantic finery and Donovan in dark formal
evening clothes. He did not wear evening
clothes with the same air of being born to
them as Jake Dominic, she mused. Despite

the faultless tailoring, the smooth material seemed to confine rather than cover the powerful shoulders, and led one to wonder at the untamed body beneath the civilized trappings. She felt a sudden surge of liquid weakness in her every limb at the sheer raw virility of the man as he prowled about the kitchen at his homely tasks.

He looked up suddenly and surprised her looking at him. His hands were arrested for a moment, as he effortlessly read the message that she was scarcely aware she was projecting.

"If you don't stop looking at me like that, I won't be responsible," he said huskily. "And I've got to talk to you."

She flushed, and looked down at her hands loosely folded on the yellow counter-top. "I don't know what you mean."

"You do, but I won't argue with you," he said roughly. "I've made a decision that I thought would suit you down to the ground, but it won't work if you keep throwing out signals. I want you too much."

She looked up in bewilderment, her doe eyes wide and asking in their frame of dark lashes.

"I've decided to give you a little more time before you fulfill your part of our little bargain," he said bluntly. "God knows how long I'll last, but I figure I can hold out for a week or so."

A cold sinking lethargy washed over her in a chilly tide that confused and frightened her. Why did she feel this sudden sense of loss?

"I see," she said quietly. "May I ask why you're being so generous?"

His mouth twisted cynically. "Perhaps I'm developing a taste for the joys of self-denial and abstention," he said dryly. "Or perhaps those big brown eyes of yours make me feel like a hunter out of season."

"That's very kind of you," she said lifelessly. "I appreciate your consideration."

"You're damn right it is," he said frowning. "I guess the truth is, I've never had to blackmail a woman to get her into bed with me before. It's leaving a bad taste in my mouth."

He suddenly reminded Brenna, rather endearingly, of a small boy who had been told that Christmas had been canceled this year.

"I thought I'd give you a chance to get to know me," he said gruffly. "Perhaps we could be friends. We seemed to be doing pretty well on the island, before you got into that damn bathtub."

Brenna hid an amused smile at the accusing tone of the statement. She wondered if he had conveniently forgotten that he had ordered her into that bathtub.

"Do you think it will work?" she asked solemnly, her eyes twinkling. She was suddenly feeling wonderfully lighthearted.

"Hell, I don't know!" he growled sourly. "But the alternate is to forget about the coffee, and I take you upstairs and don't let you out of that bedroom for a week."

"I see," she said earnestly. "Well, then perhaps we'd better try." An impish grin curved her lips, and her brown eyes were shining mischievously. "After all, I wouldn't want to take you away from your work."

There was a trace of disgruntled conjecture in the blue eyes, as Donovan took in the demure smile on Brenna's face.

"Don't get too cocky," he said warningly. "It's only a postponement, not a reprieve."

"Who knows what can happen in a week," she said breezily. "You may decide I don't appeal to you. After all, I'm not your regulation sex goddess."

"No, you're not," he agreed, his eyes suddenly dark and intense, as he came slowly forward to stand before her. There was a breathless electricity in the air, as he reached out with one finger and traced the fine contour of her cheekbone. "You're much too thin; a strong wind could blow you away. Your face is lovely, but I've seen lovelier. Except for your eyes, it's not an outstanding face." He cradled her face in his hands with a yearning tenderness. "And then you smile, and all I want to do is pick you up and carry you away somewhere, so that you'll never give that special smile to anyone but me." His lips touched hers gently. "You're much more dangerous to a man than any sex goddess, sweetheart."

She stared up, mesmerized, into his lean, tan face, feeling tears brighten her eyes and her throat constrict painfully. He was doing it again, she thought helplessly. She could fight against his blatant sex appeal, but what defense could she offer against this aching tenderness that left her conscious of an ephemeral something just out of reach.

"I think we'd better forget about the coffee tonight," he said hoarsely, as he turned away abruptly. "I've had your things put in the second bedroom on the right, at the top of the stairs. You'll forgive me if I don't show you to your room." The muscles in his back and shoulders were tense beneath the fine material of his evening jacket, as he walked over to the coffeemaker and pulled the plug from the socket.

He turned back when there was no move-

ment from the breakfast bar, and found
Brenna sitting quite still, staring at him with
dazed, dreamy eyes. "Brenna, dammit!" he
started in exasperation, then broke off as
her expression changed not a whit. "Have a
heart, love," he said huskily. "I can't take
much more."

Brenna shook her head dazedly, as if just
coming awake. She slipped from the stool,
and with a breathless, "Good night" and a
flurry of lemon chiffon, she was gone.

It was only as she was halfway up the
stairs, her heart beating with a wild exhilaration and a singing happiness surging in her
veins, that she realized what that ephemeral
element was that was causing this breathtaking delight. She was in love with Michael
Donovan.

Brenna stretched lazily, before adjusting the
vinyl lounge chair to the recline position,
not forgetting to remove her sunglasses, as
she prepared to increase the already golden
tan she had acquired in the past two weeks.
Michael had teased her unmercifully when
she had forgotten to take the glasses off,
and it had resulted in her having owl-like
rings about her eyes for two days before her
tan had evened out again.

She smiled reminiscently, a glow of contentment warming her face as she thought about the last two weeks. It had been a lovely time. Each golden day had been added like charms on a bracelet that she hoped would encircle her for an eternity. She had grown to know Michael Donovan with an intimacy that she had never thought possible. Looking on him now with the eyes of love, she found him both more difficult and simple in nature than she had first imagined.

He had kept his promise about the ultimate intimacy, but she found him to be a compulsively physical person. He was constantly touching her, holding her hand and playing idly with her fingers as he talked, stroking the silky fall of her hair in the evenings while they sat on the couch in the living room and listened to music. There were light sweet kisses and casual embraces in abundance. All were carefully controlled and designed not to upset the delicate balance of their relationship. Even on the evenings they had guests, usually members of the cast or crew of various Donovan projects at the complex, he would absently knead her shoulders as she sat comfortably at his feet by his chair in the library, as they all engaged in one of the informal bull sessions that she soon discovered were a way of life at Donovan's home.

She loved it all. After a childhood deprived of cuddling and embraces, Donovan's casual fondling made her feel warmly treasured.

Donovan did the majority of his work at home, she found. He had both an editing and projection room at the house, and there was a constant flow of people from the complex in and out of the house at all hours of the day and evening. He sometimes spent a few hours in the morning at his executive office at the complex, but most of the time he worked at the house, and his workday seemed to span most of the hours of the day and evening. He was a workaholic, as Walters had told her, and he was passionately in love with the making of films.

To her delight, she discovered that this did not necessarily shut her out of his life. After the first few lonely days, he arbitrarily ordered her into the editing room, much to the amusement of the crew. While they worked and argued and generally ignored her presence, she curled up in a chair in the corner, watching in fascination or leafing idly through a book or script. On occasion, she would look up to find Donovan looking at her with an absent smile, that she met with a blissfully contented one of her own.

In the afternoons, she usually tried to

spend time with Randy, or lazily sunbathed by the pool in a bikini, where Donovan joined her on occasion for a brief swim before he returned to work. These were the times she liked the best. When they would talk quietly, exchanging viewpoints and exploring each others minds and personalities, or just sitting in companionable silence, enjoying the warmth of the sun.

She was well aware that she owed a large measure of the mellow serenity of those days to the self-control that Donovan was exercising. Though the fact that Donovan was not used to restraining his sexual urges was painfully clear, and there were times she felt his patience was wearing dangerously thin, Donovan never made her consciously aware of the fires banked low beneath the surface.

The only cloud in this halcyon hiatus was Donovan's persistent rejection of Randy. Though not deliberately unkind to the child, the sight of him seemed to trigger a brooding moodiness in Donovan that almost invariably resulted in Brenna sending for Doris to remove the boy before the atmosphere became definitely strained. She had tentatively tried to broach the subject of his attitude once, only to be met with a steel-like hardness.

"Leave it, Brenna," he had said curtly. "I know all the logical and reasonable arguments. I realize he's an individual, and should be accepted as such. If he belonged to someone else, I'd probably be crazy about him. Hell! I like kids."

"Then why are you so unfair to Randy?" Brenna had asked huskily, her eyes bright with tears. "He's only a baby."

He had given a smothered imprecation, and kissed her gently, his hand stroking her hair with exquisite tenderness. "Because I am not rational and reasonable when it comes to you," he had said simply. "And it drives me crazy when I see him, and know that he's another man's baby and not mine. I'm trying, dammit, but it's just going to take time."

She had been very close in that moment to revealing the truth about Randy and Janine. Now that she was aware of the deep love that she had for Donovan, it was agonizingly painful to let a barrier exist that could be toppled by a few words. Surely they had grown close enough that she could put her trust in Donovan. She did not know what made her hesitate, but in the next moment Donovan was called away to the phone, and the opportunity was lost.

When Brenna first realized she loved Donovan, she went through a period of depression and sheer unadulterated panic. How had it happened, she wondered bewilderedly. Why hadn't her distrust and cynicism toward men protected her against this calamity? And if she had to fall in love with someone, why did it have to be Michael Donovan, with his penchant for noninvolvement and his reputation for being a tomcat extraordinaire?

She gradually accepted the fact that it was too late for questioning. The fact existed. She did love Michael Donovan, and in the past two weeks she had become aware that he was eminently worth loving. Not only was he brilliant and possessed of an electric charisma, but he had an unswerving honesty and directness with his associates. If he was ruthless in his dealings with those who got in his way, he was generous to a fault with his friends.

She had come to terms with her love for him now. She knew without question that though she desperately wanted his love, if that wasn't to be, she would accept what he would give her, for however long it would last. Just the experience of loving him would enrich her as an individual, and make her stronger in spirit than when she had come to him. She would have gone to bed with him gladly. That she had not offered herself was only because each day that passed strengthened their knowledge of each other, and she felt she urgently needed his friendship first if she was ever going to win anything from him but passion.

Brenna rolled over on her stomach and put her head on her folded arm, after shifting the long swatch of hair over one shoulder to expose her back to the rays of the sun. She yawned drowsily and her lids were growing deliciously heavy, when she was rudely awakened by a sharp slap on her rounded bottom.

"You look entirely too comfortable, woman," Donovan drawled. "Turn over and entertain me like a dutiful wife should."

She opened her eyes to see Michael settling in the lounge next to her. Dressed in black trunks, his tan muscular body looked lean yet powerful, the springy dark red hair on his chest lending him a sensual virility that caused a heat to flow through her body that was not from the sun.

"How dare you look so vigorous?" she said sleepily. "You were up till four this morning working with that writer on the script changes for *Wild Heritage*. And then you had breakfast with me at nine. Don't you ever get tired?"

He arched an eyebrow wickedly. "I'm glad to see you're keeping an eye on my nocturnal habits," he said teasingly. "It bodes well for the future." He shook his head in answer to her question. "I don't need much sleep. Four or five hours is more than enough. I guess it's because of my childhood. When I was working all the hours there were to get out of the slums, I always thought sleeping was a waste of time, if not my actual enemy."

She felt an urge to reach out and touch his arm, not in desire but in sympathy for the boy that was. She knew better than to give in to the impulse. Donovan was proud, and that boy had fought his battles and won them a long time ago.

She sat up and swung her legs over the side of the lounge. She leaned lazily back, bracing her weight on her stiffened arms. "How is the preproduction work going on *Wild Heritage*?" she asked casually.

"Well enough," Donovan answered. "We should be ready to start shooting next week."

"You're not directing *Heritage* are you?" she asked. "Didn't I hear you tell Jake you were giving it to that TV director who had never done a theatrical film?"

"What big ears you have, grandma," he said with a grin. "Tim Butler is a terrific director. He did fantastic things with that David and Bathsheba mini-series, and I have too many irons in the fire right now."

"Speaking of *Wild Heritage,* I have a bone to pick with you," she said severely. "I was talking to Jake about your views on method acting the other evening. When I told him what a fanatic you were on the subject, he nearly fell off the couch laughing. He said you must have been pulling my leg."

Donovan looked down at the two delectable limbs in question and murmured, "What an intriguing idea."

"Michael!" Brenna said warningly. "Why did you give me all that garbage about experience and method acting if you didn't mean it?" As she continued to think about it, her indignation grew. "Why didn't you give me Angie? I was damn good. I know I was!"

"Yes," he said lazily. "You were better than any of the others who tested for it." He leaned back, and tipped his head back like a cat arching lazily in the sun.

"Michael!" she said in exasperation.

He turned and smiled mockingly. "Jake has an exceedingly big mouth," he said calmly. "Now I suppose I'll have to confess. I made up all that tripe about method acting on the spur of the moment to give me an excuse not to hire you for Angie. I knew from the minute I saw you that I couldn't let you have it."

As she opened her mouth to protest, he quickly put his hand over her lips to silence her. "In case you hadn't noticed, there are two sexually explicit bedroom scenes, and in one Angie is nude. It's necessary for the story. There was no way I could tolerate you doing that . . . even then." His tone was grim. "I would have felt like killing someone, before the damn picture was finished."

When he removed his hand, she looked at him solemnly. "I didn't notice," she said in a small voice, a flush pinking her cheeks.

"I didn't think you had," Donovan said with a grin. "I was feeling a bit guilty about taking it away from you, when I realized Mary Durney was available. I could have my cake and eat it, too. It's going to be a hell of a good movie. I'm going to make a bundle on it."

"Egad, what a shockingly commercial mind you have," she exclaimed in mock horror, her eyes twinkling. "What about art for art's sake?"

"I'm just a bloody capitalist," he admitted, with an underlying seriousness beneath the lightness of his tone. "I consider myself an artist, and a very good one. I make the very best films of which I am capable. I'm a storyteller par excellence. In our society, the most revered reward for achievement is money, not critical acclaim, and I'll be damned if I don't wrest the greatest reward possible for my work."

She was silent for a long moment before she asked, "Have you ever not made money on one of your films?"

"Once I came pretty close," he said thoughtfully, his blue eyes reminiscent. "I was just starting out, and it was only my second film. The critics panned it and the public stayed away in droves. Everyone said it was too simple, the imagery not exotic enough."

"What did you do?" she asked curiously.

"I borrowed enough money to get me to Cannes, and entered it in the festival," he said simply. "It won best picture. Then I brought it home, and sent the actors around to every talk show on the circuit. The picture didn't win the Academy Award that year, but it was nominated." He grinned lightly. "And I made a small fortune on it."

"Tribute," Brenna said thoughtfully.

"Tribute," he agreed quietly.

They were silent in a perfect accord that lasted for a few golden moments.

"Come on, lazybones," Donovan said

briskly, rising to his feet. "I'll race you to the end of the pool."

She shook her head. "I've just been in. I'll wait for you here."

She watched as he dived cleanly from the side and did three laps in the pool, his arms cleaving the water with power and precision. When he hoisted himself out of the water at the edge of the pool, he wasn't even breathing heavily, she noticed ruefully. She threw him a towel which he caught deftly and proceeded to dry the thick mahogany hair, then his body, before wrapping the towel around his middle, and sauntering back to the chair where she was sitting.

Her eyes narrowed thoughtfully, as she watched him approach.

"You look like a gladiator at the Roman Games," she commented, her lips quirking.

"And you would have been a scandalous vestal virgin," he returned lightly, his eyes surveying her bikini-clad figure with frank enjoyment. "Did you know that the vestals were not released from their bonds of chastity until they had served for thirty years?" He sat down beside her on the lounge, his eyes suddenly intent and still. "I'm beginning to feel a definite kinship with them," he said huskily.

She looked down, her eyes shy. The air

about them was crackling with the the intensity of his feelings. Brenna was vividly conscious of her near nudity, the softness and curves and the satin smoothness of her skin that seemed erotically fashioned to be pleasing to the hard, muscular form of this man.

She didn't pretend to misunderstand him. "It's only been two weeks," she said with forced lightness.

He reached out to stroke the silky curve of her shoulder. "It seemed like two years. Why do you think I've been working so hard? I'm not used to celibacy, Brenna."

Her eyes flew to his face, and a blush dyed her cheeks at what she saw there.

"God knows, I've tried to be patient," he went on roughly. "I wanted you to come to me. I didn't want to take you. Every night when I finally did get to bed, I'd lie there aching, knowing that you were just across the hall. I've been going through hell. I can't take it anymore."

He lifted her effortlessly so that she was sitting on his knees. His mouth covered hers with an aching sweetness, and then with a groan, his lips parted hers and his tongue invaded her with a savage need. With a swift movement he rolled her over so that they were lying side by side on the recliner, his mouth open and working erotically on hers, demanding her responses. His leg urgently parted her thighs. His thighs felt rough and masculine, she thought feverishly, the fine hair caressing the smoothness of her limbs with a sensual abrasiveness.

"God, you feel so good," Donovan groaned breathlessly, burying his face in the curve of her shoulder. With shaking hands he worked at the back fastening of her bikini top, and in seconds the flimsy strip of material was removed from between their bodies. His hands reached around to curve over her swollen breasts, kneading the sensitive mounds with a rhythmic urgency that caused her to cry out with the sudden heat that shot through her body. She arched against him convulsively, her hips moving blindly in an attempt to fit herself to his loins.

He shuddered, and tore the towel from around his hips in a frantic attempt for a closer unity, and Brenna drew her breath in sharply, as she felt the taut flesh burning through the cool dampness of his trunks. His mouth was on one taut nipple, his tongue teasing it maddeningly while his thumb flicked its sensitive mate, until she was writhing, her breath coming in little gasps. "Please," she begged. "Michael, please . . ."

One hand traveled from her breast to the tense muscles of her stomach, stroking and rubbing the silken skin caressingly, before slipping down beneath the bikini briefs, his other hand loosening the ties at her hips. He lifted and threw back his head, the cords standing out on his strong throat. "God! I want you! Now!" he said, tormented. He closed his eyes, his hands still moving compulsively on her body.

He drew a deep breath, and a convulsive shudder shook his body. Suddenly he rolled away from her, and was on his feet beside the recliner, his hands clenched into fists. He looked down at her, his chest heaving with the effort he was making for control.

She looked up at him, her bare breasts moving rapidly with the same emotion that was wracking him.

"Cover yourself!" he said thickly. "Or so help me, I'll take you right here and now, and I won't give a damn how public it is."

She sat up slowly and looked around for something to cover herself. The bikini top seemed to have disappeared, and she was looking around for it vaguely, when Donovan gave a smothered imprecation and reached down for the towel he had discarded. He threw it to her impatiently.

She clutched it obediently, tucking it beneath her arms, not realizing how provocative the pose was.

Donovan's face was set in harsh lines, his blue eyes burning with flames not yet subsided. "I've got appointments and meetings set up all day and most of the evening," he said grimly, his gaze drawn compulsively to the high curves of her breasts beneath the towel. "So you have another reprieve. It's your last one, Brenna, and for only twenty-four hours." He lifted his hand as if to ward off her protests and arguments, though, in truth, she was not saying a word, just gazing at him with wide, luminous eyes.

"I can't help it if you're not ready, or if you want more time," he said harshly. "I've waited long enough." He turned on his heel, and strode away toward the house, aggressiveness and belligerence in every step.

Brenna settled back on the recliner, still clutching the towel and gazed after him, a loving amusement in her eyes and the deliciously contented smile of a cat who'd just been given the deed to the dairy.

NINE

"I'll be back before five," Doris Charles said worriedly. "You're sure you don't mind taking care of him for a few hours? After all, I had a day off just two days ago. I feel a little guilty taking off again so soon."

Brenna grinned. "Remember to whom you're speaking. I'm the Cinderella girl who never even dreamed she'd have a nanny for Randy only a month ago. Besides, a trip to the dentist isn't exactly a wild spree. Haven't you ever heard of sick benefits?"

"Well, if you're sure . . ." Doris said doubtfully, and Brenna briskly assured her that she was quite sure, and with a little more coaxing, Doris Charles was persuaded to leave.

Brenna shook her head ruefully, as she picked Randy up in preparation for a trip to the sandbox in the corner of the patio. Sometimes she thought Doris was a little too dedicated to Randy. That infected wisdom tooth must have been excruciating, yet she had put off having it pulled for almost a day, because she didn't want to leave Randy with his own mother. She would enjoy having Randy to herself again, Brenna thought happily, and Doris would surely be back in time to take Randy over while she dressed for dinner. The note Michael had left her at breakfast had said he'd join her for dinner at eight.

She had not seen Michael since he had left her at the pool yesterday, but Mrs. Haskins had told her this morning that he had gone to the complex to see Mr. Walters. He would probably be closeted with Monty most of the day, and lucky to be home for dinner, she thought anxiously. Then her frown cleared miraculously as she remembered Donovan's lovemaking by the pool yesterday. She had an idea it would take more than a business meeting to keep him from keeping their appointment tonight.

She put Randy down in the sandbox and handed him his pail and shovel. She settled down in a nearby lounge chair with a script that Michael had given her two days ago with a brief comment that the feminine lead had possibilities. She had only gotten through the third scene, but she could already see what he meant. She was soon absorbed in the snappy dialogue of the romantic comedy.

"What a domestic scene. It really touches my paternal heart." The tone was sarcastic and the voice was that of Paul Chadeaux.

Brenna looked up, shocked, her face paling as she realized it really was Chadeaux standing before her, sartorically perfect in a dark blue lounge suit, his gray eyes ugly.

"What are you doing here? Who let you in?" she asked hoarsely.

Chadeaux sat down on the lounge chair opposite her and answered coolly, "Your housekeeper was very obliging. I explained that I was a friend of yours, and she told me to go right on through to the terrace."

It was an understandable error, Brenna thought numbly. Chadeaux was well dressed and personable, and Mrs. Haskins was accustomed to a constant flow of guests coming and going in this house.

Chadeaux was gazing critically at the golden-haired baby playing contentedly in the sandbox. "He's a good-looking kid," he said impersonally. "He has the Chadeaux coloring."

"Many children are very blond when they are young," Brenna answered coolly. "Their color frequently darkens as they grow older."

He shot her a poisonous glance. "You have all the answers, don't you? You and those smart-alec lawyers your husband turned loose on me. It was pretty clever of you to put a noose around Donovan, and get him to do your dirty work."

Brenna's lips tightened. "We have nothing further to talk about, Paul," she said tersely. "Please leave."

Chadeaux smiled nastily. "You think you've won, don't you, little sister? Well, don't count on it," he said. "Donovan may have enough clout to put a spoke in my wheel, but I'm not about to be beaten by some upstart movie mogul." His face twisted balefully.

"You have no choice in the matter," Brenna said, moistening her lips nervously.

"You're wrong. There's always an angle; you just have to find it." Chadeaux's gray eyes were narrowed and sly. "And I've figured the angle, little sister. It's all very simple." He rose lazily to his feet. "You and I and junior, over there, are going on a little trip. We're going to a nice private place where the two of us can 'negotiate.'"

She stared at him incredulously. "We're not going anywhere with you," she said flatly. "Why should we?"

"Because I'm a desperate man, little

sister," he said venomously. "The men to whom I owe money are not very understanding of custody battles and legal delays. If I don't produce their money by next Tuesday, I'm in big trouble."

He reached out and grabbed her wrist brutally, jerking her to her feet. "Get the kid. We're leaving right now!"

She struggled futilely in an attempt to break his hold. "You're crazy," she said furiously. "Do you think you can just drag us out of here? Do you think I won't fight you? All I have to do is call and Mrs. Haskins or one of the servants will be right here."

Chadeaux's grip tightened agonizingly on her wrist, and she cried out in pain. "But you won't call," he said menacingly. "Because you have a certain fondness for that sweet little tyke of mine."

Brenna could feel the blood drain from her face as she stared at him in horror. "What do you mean?" she whispered hoarsely, her eyes wide and frightened.

"Children are very vulnerable," he said softly, and his gaze traveled significantly to the swimming pool a few yards away.

"My God! What kind of monster are you?" she said, fear making her sick. "He's your own child."

"I told you I was desperate," he snarled.

"I'm not stupid enough to murder the little brat, but I'm not above making him quite uncomfortable if I have to." He smiled unpleasantly. "But I'm not going to have to do that, am I, Brenna? You couldn't stand knowing that you're to blame for causing the little angel any pain, could you?"

"No, you mustn't hurt him," Brenna said sharply. "I'll go with you. Just don't hurt Randy!"

"I thought you'd be reasonable," he said smugly. "Now, let's get going. My car is parked in the driveway out front. I see there's a path that circles the house. We won't need to go back inside."

"I need to change," she said quickly, "and I'll have to get some things for Randy." If she could see Mrs. Haskins, perhaps she could signal her in some way, she thought desperately.

Chadeaux shook his head. "Do you think I'm stupid?" he asked arrogantly. He casually gazed at her lilac slacks and white sun top. "You're okay as you are, and I can buy anything the kid needs on the way. I'm not about to let you be tempted to make a dumb move, and start shouting for help. Now, get the kid before I lose my temper." He released her arm with a little shove. "Move!"

Brenna backed slowly away from him, rubbing her bruised wrist and thinking frantically, trying to see a way out of this horror that would pose no danger to Randy. Chadeaux was a weak, self-indulgent man but in this case he had the desperate viciousness of a cornered rat. She had no doubt that Chadeaux meant what he said when he threatened Randy. She knew from experience how callously cruel he could be.

"Shall I do it myself?" Chadeaux asked with soft menace. "If you force me to, I won't be as gentle with him as you will."

"No, please," she said, alarmed. She walked over to the sandbox and lifted the protesting baby, cuddling him protectively.

"Good," Chadeaux said grimly. "Now, keep on being a smart girl, and we'll get along fine."

His hand beneath her elbow, he propelled her quickly across the terrace and down the stone walkway that encircled the house.

Brenna searched wildly for some sign of the gardener or Bob, her driver, but neither were in evidence. When they reached the red Buick rental car, she was forced to admit to herself that if she were going to get out of this dangerous predicament, she could not rely on outside help. She must find some way to save Randy herself.

■ ■ ■ ■

They were a few miles out of Twin Pines, approaching the highway when Brenna made an attempt to reason with Chadeaux for the last time. "You do realize this is kidnapping?" she asked quietly. "You could go to jail for a long time. If you'll just let us go, I promise I'll forget all about it."

"How generous," Chadeaux jeered scornfully. "As it happens, I won't need your generosity. After I get what I want, I will let you go and you won't dare go to the police."

They had reached the highway now and, to her surprise, he didn't turn south toward the California border, but north.

"We're not going to Chadeaux Park?" she asked with some trepidation. She had been hoping she could appeal to the more reasonable members of the Chadeaux family.

"Randy and I will be going there later," Chadeaux said. "Right now, we're headed toward Portland. I want to be close to the airport, so that I can get a plane immediately." He shot her a mocking glance. "After you prove how cooperative you can be."

Brenna shook her head. "I'll never let you have Randy," she said quietly.

"We'll see, little sister," he said softly.

"We'll see."

It was almost twilight, and they had reached the outskirts of Portland, when Chadeaux suddenly pulled off the highway. A blue neon sign blinking on and off announced their arrival at the Pinetree Motel. Chadeaux drew up before the small office with a lighted vacancy sign in the large glass picture window.

It was a singularly unimpressive establishment, Brenna noticed drearily. The U-shaped motel units were constructed of gray brick and cedar. Green shutters framed the windows of each individual unit, and the faded and peeling paint gave the motel a generally seedy air.

"This will have to do," Chadeaux said briefly. He reached for Randy who had been lulled to sleep by the motion of the car. "I'll just take the kid in with me when I register. I don't think you'll have any bright ideas about taking off while I have him."

Chadeaux returned to the car in a short time, and drove to the far end of the court to a unit with a large brass number seven on the door.

"My lucky number," he announced with satisfaction, parking directly in front of the door. "Everything is going to turn out just fine, little sister."

Brenna hugged Randy's body to her nervously as Chadeaux indicated that she should get out of the car.

Chadeaux unlocked the door and pushed her in ahead of him, shutting the door behind him.

Brenna looked around her wearily. The room was small and shabby, with the regulation twin beds and the combination desk-dresser that was common to small-town motels everywhere. At least the room looked fairly clean, Brenna thought tiredly.

She laid Randy down on one of the beds, gently brushing a lock of hair from his forehead.

She turned to Chadeaux, and said, "It's past his dinnertime. He must have something to eat."

"He's asleep," Chadeaux said, with a shrug. "He'll be all right for a while." He removed his jacket and threw it on the bed beside Randy. "In the meantime, we can come to an understanding."

Brenna looked at him steadily. "I don't know what you expect to accomplish, but whatever it is, it's not going to work, Paul."

A flicker of anger flashed in the shallow gray eyes. "It had better work," he said malevolently. "Or you're going to be very, very sorry, little sister."

"Stop calling me that!" Brenna snapped, her nerves raw and quivering from the worry and tension of the past hours.

"I'll call you what I please, bitch," he snarled. "I've had enough of your insolence. Now you're going to do what you're told."

With three strides he was across the room. His hands fastened with brutal ferocity on her slender shoulders, and he watched her face with savage enjoyment as he slowly tightened his grip until the pain was excruciating. She cried out in agony.

"Shall I tell you what you're going to do, little sister?" he said tauntingly. "You're going to sit down at that desk over there, and you're going to write out a complete account of Randy's birth, naming me as the father and Janine as the mother, and confessing all the details of Janine's little plot. You're going to give names, dates, and places, so that it will stand up in any court in the country."

Brenna shook her head, her face twisted in pain from the grip that felt as if it were a medieval torture clamp.

"I won't do it," she gasped, tears running down her face. "I'll never let you have Randy."

"Dammit! You will!" Chadeaux snarled furiously, shaking her back and forth, like a dog with a rag doll. He spun her around, and twisted her arm behind her back as he forced her across the room to the desk. As he pulled the desk chair out, his grip loosened fractionally, and with a lightning movement Brenna jerked free and whirled away from him. She backed away, her breast heaving, her eyes wild with fright.

"Damn you!" Chadeaux swore furiously and charged after her, grabbing her once more by the shoulders and trying futilely to subdue her frantic struggles as desperation lent her additional strength. Their struggles had led them to the edge of the vacant bed near the desk, when Chadeaux saw a way of gaining the advantage.

Using the weight of his body, he overbalanced her and she fell heavily onto the bed, striking her head on the wooden headboard. Blinding pain was followed by a moment of darkness, and she went limp beneath Chadeaux's weight. With a swift, satisfied exclamation he pinned her arms above her head, holding her helpless.

He looked down at her in triumph, breathing hard. Suddenly his expression changed, taking on a lustful malevolence that frightened her more than his anger. His gaze went lingeringly over her tousled hair and the top that was now barely covering the tips of her heaving breasts. He ran his tongue over his full lips and his eyes narrowed into gleaming silver slits.

"Suddenly I'm not in a hurry for that affidavit," he drawled thickly. "I think I'll just see if you're as good as your sister." His mouth pressed down brutally on hers, bruising the soft inner flesh against her teeth, as she frantically moved her head from side to side to escape him.

"Get off her, Chadeaux." The words were said with a soft menace that held all the danger of a bared stiletto.

Chadeaux froze, and Brenna drew a breath of infinite thanksgiving.

Donovan held the key to the room in his hand. Obviously he'd used his influence to get it from the motel office. Now he hurled it furiously to the floor and lunged across the room. He jerked Chadeaux up from the bed, throwing him violently against the wall. He followed, his powerful hands squeezing the collar of Chadeaux's shirt into a stranglehold, causing congested color to mount in Chadeaux's frightened face.

"Wait!" Chadeaux gasped desperately, "Listen to me!"

Donovan's face was a mask of rage, his eyes the flaming blue of the fires of hell. "No, you listen. If you say one more word,

229

I'm going to beat you senseless." Donovan grated, between his teeth. "I may still do it, even if you don't."

Brenna sat up dazedly, her eyes fixed in fascination on Donovan. She didn't blame Chadeaux for his almost abject terror. There was such an aura of rage about Donovan that it was as if he were surrounded by an invisible wall of flame.

Donovan's words came with the soft rapidity of a machine gun. "I'm going to tell you this once, Chadeaux, and never again, so you listen carefully. You're never to see my wife again. You're never to talk to her on the telephone. You're never to write to her. You're most particularly not to lay a finger on her again. If you do, I swear you'll wish you had never been born! Do you understand?"

Chadeaux nodded, his eyes bulging, as he gasped helplessly for air.

Donovan turned to Brenna, and her breath caught. She shrank back against the headboard at the white hot fury in his face.

"Get up, and get out of here," he ordered harshly. "Bob Phillips is waiting outside. Take Randy out to him."

Brenna scrambled off the bed, experiencing a few moments of dizziness that caused her to falter momentarily before rushing around to pick up Randy from the bed and hurry to the open door.

Donovan was waiting there, his face white and set. He hesitated a moment, then, as if unable to resist the impulse, he turned back and strode to where Chadeaux was cringing against the far wall.

"I told you I might do it anyway," he said coolly, and struck him a bruising blow to the chin. Chadeaux grunted once, his eyes glazing over, and then slid slowly down the wall, unconscious.

Without giving him another glance, Donovan turned and walked away, grabbing Brenna by the elbow and sweeping her grimly from the room.

As he had said, Bob Phillips was standing by the Mercedes, a worried frown on his craggy face. He carefully avoided Brenna's eyes as they approached. "Everything okay?" he asked Donovan.

Donovan nodded tersely. Taking the sleeping Randy from Brenna, he handed him to Phillips. "Doris Charles will be at the Portland airport by now. I radioed Monty to have her flown here over an hour ago."

Brenna felt her head whirling in bewilderment, as Phillips put Randy carefully in the front seat of the car. Things had been moving too fast since Donovan had appeared on the scene. She took an automatic step toward the child, and Donovan's hand tightened on her elbow. "No," he clipped harshly. "You come with me."

He led her to an ancient Chevy pickup truck parked a few spaces away. She allowed him to help her into the vehicle with a meek docility that was foreign to her. She felt only a dull curiosity as he put the truck in gear and with much coughing and sputtering eased it onto the highway.

"Where are we going?" she asked remotely. She wished vaguely that the fierce throbbing in her head would stop.

"I landed the 'copter at a private airport about three miles from here," he said shortly. "I rented the truck from a kid who services the airplanes."

Brenna nodded weakly, leaning her head against the back of the seat. She closed her eyes to shut out the brilliance of the oncoming headlights that only increased the stabbing pain behind her eyes. She vaguely realized that there were many questions still unanswered, but she had no energy or strength to ask them at the moment. It was enough, for now, that Randy and she were safe and on their way home to Twin Pines.

Donovan seemed to have a similar disinclination to talk, and the transfer from the pickup to the helicopter was made in virtual silence. It wasn't until they were underway for almost twenty minutes that she realized from the mirrored shifting horizon that they were over water. The shock of the discovery jolted her sharply out of the haze of pain and weariness that had enveloped her since she had first seen Donovan at the motel.

"There's some mistake," Brenna shouted over the noise of the rotors, pointing at the still waters of the Pacific below them.

Donovan's mouth twisted. "No mistake," he said with a coolness that was belied by his taut, chiseled face and burning eyes. "We're going to the island."

Brenna shook her head. "We can't," she protested in confusion. "I have to get back to Randy." Somehow in the bewilderment and exhaustion of that moment, the urgency to be with Randy, and reassure herself that he was blessedly safe and secure was paramount.

Donovan shot her a brief glance that had the force of a blow. "I realize how devoted you are to your son," he said coldly. "He's being flown back to Twin Pines, and will be well taken care of. You, however, are going to the island," he finished inexorably.

She shook her head in dejected bewilderment. She couldn't understand why Donovan was so displeased with her. It was not her fault that she had been forced to go with Chadeaux. Even if Donovan had been put to a certain amount of trouble on her behalf, he still did not have to be so irascible. Her mouth twisted wryly at the blatant understatement. He was obviously in a white-hot rage. But why were they going to the island, she wondered uneasily.

When she hesitantly ventured the question to the grim stranger beside her, she received no answer other than a contemptuous smile that did nothing to put her mind at rest.

He wasn't any more communicative after they had landed the helicopter on the island, and made their way through the woods, their path lit by the powerful beam of Donovan's flashlight. His pace was fast and relentless, and he made no concession for her smaller stride, merely propelling her ahead of him with a determination that gave her neither breath nor strength for protests or questions.

It was not until they had reached the chalet, and he had shut the door and flashed on the overhead light, that he turned to regard her white face, tousled hair, and rapidly heaving breast with cool appraisal. "You look like you could use a drink," he said impersonally, crossing to the portable bar and pouring her a small brandy. He returned to hand it to her with an expressionless face.

She took a small sip of the amber liquid, and made a face at the obnoxious taste, though it did feel glowingly warm going down. After he had given her the glass, he went back to the stone fireplace and was in the process now of building a fire with swift economical movements. She watched him for a moment, then went over to the scarlet couch and curled up in one corner of it, her legs tucked beneath her like a small child. Indeed, she felt like a child, she thought wearily. One who had been punished unfairly, and who now still had to face the incomprehensible anger of grown-ups.

Donovan had succeeded in bringing a brisk crackling blaze to life, and he turned from where he was kneeling to regard her once more with that inexplicable air of cold antagonism. "Feeling better?" he asked carelessly, and as she nodded silently, he rose and removed his dark suit jacket and tie, throwing them both carelessly on the velvet arm chair. He rolled up his sleeves baring his powerfully muscled forearms, and, crossing back to the bar, made himself a drink.

He did not join her on the couch, but returned to the fireplace to stand with his back to the flames, his legs spread apart and the orange glow a fiery aureole around him. He looked one with the flames, Brenna thought hazily, the combination of the brandy and shock making her dreamily fanciful. He was Lucifer, springing from his fiery kingdom. The vibrant vitality that was always present in him seemed to be almost a visible and dangerous force tonight. Her tortured nerves, that had begun to relax infinitesimally with the soothing effect of the brandy and warmth of the fire, tightened warily as she met the impenetrable blue eyes of the man opposite her.

She brushed a swatch of hair away from her cheek, and moistened her lips nervously. "How did you know where to find us?" she asked falteringly.

The line of Donovan's lips hardened, and he finished half of his drink in a quick swallow. "I suppose like most women, you're enamored of explanations, and must have everything laid out for you," he said cynically. "I wouldn't probe too deeply into my discovery that you were gone, if I were you. My emotions are still a bit raw, and I'm trying hard to control my less than civilized impulses."

She looked at him bewilderedly. "I don't understand," she said slowly, her brown eyes widening.

"Still playing the innocent?" he asked derisively. "You do it very well, Brenna, but the game is over." He took another swallow of his drink. "However, I'm willing to satisfy your curiosity." He leaned indolently against the side of the fireplace.

"Bob Phillips was in the garage, tinkering with the Mercedes, when he saw you get into the car with Chadeaux. He hadn't been notified that you were going out today, so he called through to my office on the car phone to check." Donovan's mouth twisted bitterly.

"I recognized the description of Chadeaux at once, and told Phillips to follow you and report back to me on the CB radio. I was at the airstrip in ten minutes, and have been in constant contact with Phillips on the ground ever since. When it became evident that you were headed for Portland, I radioed Monty to pick up Doris Charles and get her there on the double."

Brenna rubbed her head wearily, her face still puzzled. "But why would Phillips notify you just because he wasn't told I was going out?"

Donovan shrugged. "It was his job to keep

track of you," he said coolly.

Brenna put her glass down very carefully on the end table beside her. "Do you mean that Phillips wasn't a chauffeur at all?" she asked quietly. "That he was some sort of spy with orders to report to you?"

"Not a spy, a bodyguard," Donovan replied incredibly. "When you married me, you automatically became the target of all sorts of undesirables, from kidnappers to cranks who think they have a grudge against me for one reason or another. I was trying to protect you." He smiled mirthlessly. "I trusted you. We had a bargain. You're to be complimented. You were very convincing. I don't often trust a woman's word."

Brenna flinched at the stinging sarcasm of his tone, and the smoldering anger that couldn't be mistaken in his eyes. She began to feel a rising sense of aggravation at Donovan's antagonistic attitude. She had played the victim long enough in this scenario. First with that swine Chadeaux, and now with Donovan and his incomprehensible sniping.

"I'm a bit tired of your sarcasm and innuendos, Michael," she said lifting her chin. "I have nothing to be ashamed of, and if you have some complaint, I wish you'd speak up."

"I believe the time for speech is past," Donovan said harshly, as he replaced his glass on the bar. "We have nothing further to discuss, Brenna. It's time for the payment of debts." In two long strides he had reached her, pulling her to her feet and into his arms with an explosive release of the savagery that had smoldered just beneath the surface. His mouth crushed hers with a brutal strength that bruised her lips and robbed her of breath. She grew faint and dizzy as it seemed to continue interminably.

When his lips left hers they were both breathing hard, and she leaned weakly against him, her shaking legs unwilling to support her.

"What was the matter, Brenna?" Donovan said savagely, his blue eyes burning. "When I told you it was time you kept your bargain, did you panic at the thought of giving yourself to anyone but that miserable bastard, who used you and then deserted you? Did you decide you wanted him after all?" His mouth covered hers again as if he were draining the very life force from her. "Did you phone him yesterday after I left you, and tell him to come for you?" he asked harshly, as his hands fastened in her hair and pulled her head back roughly.

"No, it's not true," Brenna whimpered.

Never in her wildest imaginings had she thought that Donovan would believe she had gone with Chadeaux willingly. She put her hands against his chest protestingly. "You must believe me, Michael," she said huskily, looking up at him entreatingly. "I didn't go with him of my own accord. He forced me."

"What truly incredible eyes you have," Donovan said mockingly, his face hard. "They have the gentleness and innocence of a young doe. You might even have been able to fool me again, if I hadn't seen you on that bed with Chadeaux." The memory of that scene caused his face to darken with such primitive rage, that Brenna felt the first thrill of real fear course through her. "God! I wish I'd killed him," he said hoarsely.

"I was fighting him," Brenna insisted desperately. "We fell . . ." He cut her off with a kiss that was even more savage than the ones that had gone on before. When he released her, she knew with a feeling of hopelessness that he had gone beyond reasoning.

"Shut up!" Donovan said huskily, his eyes wild. "He was making love to you. Phillips said you got into the car willingly. You even sent Doris Charles away for the afternoon so that you wouldn't have to make any

240

explanations about taking Randy away."

Brenna closed her eyes. It all fitted together so neatly, she thought wearily, and it formed such a completely erroneous and incriminating picture.

How was she to convince Donovan of the truth, when suddenly she was too tired to think coherently? Her head was aching intolerably, and her knees were shaking and weak with reaction to this final strain on her nerves. She knew she must try to convince Donovan how mistaken he was, but the lassitude that was slowly enveloping her made the effort seem superhuman in scope.

"No more arguments?" Donovan asked grimly. "Good." He shifted his hold and scooped her up in his arms, and headed for the spiral staircase. As he passed the light-switch, he hit it, plunging the chalet into darkness that was relieved only by the flickering light from the fire.

As Donovan negotiated the stairs, Brenna tried desperately to muster the energy to protest. This was all wrong, she realized dimly. The gossamer fabric of trust and friendship they had woven so painstakingly was now rent and torn, and Donovan's savage jealousy was threatening to destroy the pitiful remnants that remained. He carried her to the king-sized bed and placed her on the silken counterpane, then he straightened and started to undo the buttons of his white shirt.

He looked down at her, a dark anonymous shadow whose grim, taut features were occasionally illuminated by the upward surge of the flickering firelight. "I thought our first night together should be spent here, under the circumstances," he said mockingly, as he stripped off the shirt and threw it aside. "I find it most fitting that the consummation of our marriage should be in surroundings that have witnessed a multitude of similar meaningless and shallow interludes." He was swiftly stripping off the rest of his clothes, the firelight playing across the powerful shoulders and pectoral muscles of his chest.

Vulcan! she thought dimly, from some distant primal memory, as he joined her on the bed. His hands were deft and experienced as he brushed away her protesting hands, and drew the white suntop over her head, loosening the front closing of her bra with cool efficiency.

Knowing that her remonstrances would have no more effect than a flimsy canoe before a tidal wave, she felt she had to try once more. "Please, Michael," she whispered huskily. "Not like this."

"Yes, precisely like this," he said thickly. "If you expected gentleness or courtly passion, forget it. You've forfeited the right to anything but this." His hands had removed the lilac slacks, and dispensed with the minute bikini panties that were the last barrier between them. Brenna felt a flash of shame send a burning blush over her entire body, as his eyes ran over her naked beauty in almost impersonal appraisal.

"I'm going to use you, Brenna," he said hoarsely. "I'm going to use this lovely body of yours in every way I know how, and when I've finished, I'm going to do it all over again. I'm going to drown myself in you to the point of satiation, and when I've rid myself of this crazy obsession I have for you, I'm going to kick that lovely tail right out of my life and hope to God I don't have to look into those lying eyes ever again."

He pulled her close, the touch of his warm vibrant flesh against her own waking her from the dreamy lassitude that had enfolded her like a warm blanket. She reacted helplessly, as she always did, to the magnetism of his powerful body. Though his words lacerated her spirit, her flesh recognized only that this was Michael, the man she loved, and so there must be a response.

As their bodies touched, Donovan's coolness vanished as if it had never existed. His body hardened against hers, as he buried his head in her shoulder, a convulsive shudder rippling through his large frame. "Damn you!" he groaned brokenly. "Why is it that I only have to touch you, to turn on like a teenager with his first woman."

His lips covered hers, his tongue invading her to ravish her mouth as his hands were ravishing her body. He was memorizing every line and curve. His hands caressing and branding at the same time, so that she felt that after tonight there wouldn't be an inch of her that was not known and possessed by him. His mouth was at her swelling breasts, and then on the softness of her belly, before returning to her mouth again in a fever of desire.

She arched against him, no longer caring how this sensual witchery had started. She wanted only completion. The desires they felt had been banked low for too long. She could feel the need for him burn hot in every vein until she was gasping and moving helplessly, her hands running first in compulsive caresses over his smooth, muscular shoulders only to bury themselves in the thick crisp hair at the nape of his neck.

His knee parted her thighs and he knelt above her, his hands filling themselves with her breasts. His hair-roughened chest was heaving and his blue eyes glazed with emotion, as he looked down into her flushed face and glowing eyes.

"I want to devour you," he growled thickly. "I've never wanted a woman like this in my life."

Brenna was one throbbing, pulsing entity as she writhed beneath his tormenting hands. Dimly she was aware that there was something she should tell him. She tried, "Please," she gasped. "I must tell you . . ."

"Too late," he muttered hoarsely. "Too late for anything but this." And his hips plunged forward ruthlessly.

Brenna gave a muffled scream at the hot piercing jolt of pain that wracked her with shocking suddenness. Her hands, that had been caressing, now tried frantically to repulse the intruding body that was suddenly stiff and still above her.

"My God!" Donovan swore, his eyes stunned and unbelieving as he looked down at her pain-filled eyes.

"Please. Let me go," she whispered, her hands pushing at him futilely.

He closed his eyes, his face taut with the battle he was waging. When his eyes opened, they were glazed and desperate. "I can't," he groaned. "God! I can't do it. I promise

I'll make it good for you, sweetheart."

He started to move with exquisite care and patience, and he kept his word. Soon the pain was gone, lost in a rapturous vortex of sensation that seemed to be both the beginning and the end of all sensual pleasure. As she began to respond, meeting thrust for thrust with wild passion, he forgot his caution and, holding her close, he plunged again and again, his voice murmuring hotly in her ear. "God, you're so tight, sweetheart. That's it, move with me, love. Put your hands on me. Touch me, Brenna."

The passionate litany was as much an aphrodisiac as the sweetness of his lips, that moved to caress the curve of her ear and the sensitive cords of her neck. She had never known such spiraling pleasure could build to this unknown dimension that was almost painful in its intensity. It continued to build until she felt lost in rapture, before the spiral shattered in a blinding explosion that left her panting and clinging desperately to Michael, her nails buried in his shoulder, as he collapsed helplessly against her in an agony of satisfaction.

Her arms held his shuddering body firmly and tenderly. She received almost as much pleasure out of the knowledge that the supreme enjoyment of her body had brought the powerful man to this pitch of dependent need, as she had derived out of her own sexual fulfillment.

He moved off her slowly, his breathing still rapid but his heartbeat slowing as he settled on his back, his arm curved possessively around her.

Michael reached down and pulled a white fur throw from the foot of the bed. He tucked it around them, changing his position so that her head was nestled in the curve of his shoulder, her shining brown hair splayed over his chest.

Brenna nestled contentedly closer, feeling as delightfully relaxed and drowsy as a kitten. She yawned, her heavy eyelids closing irresistibly.

"Don't get too comfortable," Michael advised firmly, his deep voice rumbling beneath her ear. "You have quite a few explanations to make."

Her eyes flew open as the realization struck her. She had been so lost in the rapturous euphoria of her first experience with physical love, that she had forgotten everything but the pleasure of giving herself to Michael in this exquisite fashion. But now it was brought home to her that Michael knew!

She stiffened, and would have raised her

head to look at him, but his hand instinctively closed on her hair in jealous possession, holding her prisoner in his arms. "Talk," he ordered briskly. "I don't believe I've ever had a virgin before, but the condition is quite unmistakable."

Brenna was glad that her head was still buried in Donovan's shoulder, as the warm color rushed to her face. "I suppose you want to know about Randy?" she mumbled.

"I think I have some cause to be curious," Michael said dryly. "I believe the last recorded case of Immaculate Conception was almost two thousand years ago."

She drew a deep breath, and then said with a rush, "Randy is not my child."

"I guessed that," Donovan said ironically, his hand idly stroking her silky hair. "However, I would like to know the identity of the mother of the child I'm claiming to have fathered."

"My sister Janine," Brenna said quietly.

As briefly as possible she related the circumstances of Randy's birth and her subsequent guardianship, as well as Chadeaux's plan to gain custody of Randy and the details of the abduction today.

Michael's hand on her hair paused in its stroking action, and she felt his body stiffen with anger. "And may I ask why you didn't tell me all this when I suggested our little bargain?" he asked with steely softness. "Surely you realized you'd have to be honest with me when we went to bed. Or did you think you could postpone paying off indefinitely?"

"No," she protested indignantly, wriggling away from him and sitting up. She was unaware in her agitation, that the coverlet had dropped to her waist revealing two enticing pink nipples, peeping out from the tangle of brown satin hair. "I wanted to go to bed with you. It was you who suggested the postponement." She ran her fingers through her hair wearily. "I don't know why I didn't tell you. I was frightened and upset. Randy is all the family I have."

"You didn't trust me," Donovan said sharply. "What the hell did you think I'd do, turn the child over to that bastard?"

"You didn't like Randy," Brenna said reluctantly, not looking at him. "I couldn't take the chance."

Donovan began to swear fluently under his breath. "I never said I had a personal dislike for the child," he said between his teeth. "Of all the muddle, addle-brained, completely asinine bit of reasoning, you take the prize."

Brenna tilted her head defiantly. "He was

my responsibility," she said defensively. "How could I be sure what you would do? I hardly knew you."

"You knew me well enough to be willing to jump in bed with me," he said caustically, levering himself up into a sitting position. Even in the dimness of the firelit room, she could see the flicker of anger in his eyes. "But you didn't know me well enough to trust me to protect a helpless child!"

"I wasn't willing to jump into bed with you," Brenna said stung. "You gave me no choice."

Donovan's smile was coolly cynical. "You didn't want a choice," he drawled. "You wanted it as much as I did. I just gave you the excuse you needed." His eyes were strangely brooding, as he smiled mirthlessly, his gaze raking over the tempting beauty of her bared breasts and slim waist. He shrugged as his hands came out to clasp her slender shoulders. "Why should I care if I have your confidence?" he asked bitterly. "I have what I bargained for."

As his hands tightened on her shoulders to pull her into his arms, Brenna flinched and gave a cry of pain.

"What the hell?" Michael ejaculated, startled. He fumbled with the bedside lamp, and suddenly the room was filled with light.

"My God!" he brushed her hair gently away from her shoulders, revealing the livid, purple bruise marks on the satin skin. Michael's face was white and set, his eyes sick, as he asked hoarsely, "Did I do that?"

She looked up at him startled, her eyes wide. "No, of course you didn't," she assured him quickly. "It was Paul Chadeaux," she said ruefully. "He wasn't overly gentle in his attempts to get me to sign that affidavit."

Donovan muttered an obscene imprecation, and reached out to touch a bruise with gentle fingers. "I should have killed him," he said grimly. "What other damage did the bastard do to you?"

Brenna was suddenly frightened by the deadly anger mirrored in Donovan's eyes. "Nothing, really," she said deprecatingly. "I hit my head on the headboard when we fell on the bed, but it only hurt for a moment." She touched the side of her head gingerly.

Donovan brushed her hair aside until he found a sizable lump. She flinched as he touched the swelling, and Michael's mouth tightened ominously. "It must have hurt like hell. You're lucky you don't have a concussion." His electric blue eyes narrowed dangerously. "God! I wish I had him here now."

"It's over now. Let's forget it," Brenna said nervously.

"Yes, you forget it," Donovan said absently, his eyes thoughtful. "You've suffered enough. I'll take care of it."

"Michael, no," she protested firmly. "I'm the one who suffered injury, and if any redress is to be exacted, it would be up to me to do so. This isn't the Middle Ages, dammit. I won't have you rushing around fighting my battles as if I was some idiotic, simpering damsel in distress."

Donovan's lips quirked, and there was a flicker of amusement on his taut face. "Sorry, darling. Women's lib is out in this case," he said mockingly. "I warned you that I take care of my own." His hand slid down her shoulder to cup her breast, his eyes noting her suddenly indrawn breath with a gleam of satisfaction.

"Don't worry, I'm not going to take Chadeaux apart with my bare hands, as much as I'd enjoy it. I'll find another and more permanent way of dealing with him. You can be sure he won't ever bother you again." There was absolute assurance in Donovan's voice and Brenna shivered at the ruthless glint in his eyes.

His expression became moody as he stared into her apprehensive face. "Poor Brenna;

you're a frightened lamb in a world of ravening wolves," he said soberly. "We men haven't treated you very well in your young life, have we, love? A father who deserted you. Chadeaux causing the death of your sister, and saddling you with a child to raise." His face clouded. "Even I ended up by practically raping you. How can anyone condemn you for hating the lot of us?"

Brenna looked at him helplessly. How could she tell him it wasn't hate she felt for him, but love. Even in the throes of passion he had never indicated that he felt anything for her but a wild, obsessive desire of the flesh. To confess her own feelings, when she knew he did not share them, would leave her open and vulnerable to the most agonizing of rejections. Perhaps he was right, and she had been hurt too much in the past to put much faith in lady luck handing her the prize of Donovan's love.

Donovan's expression hardened, and his mouth curved cynically. "No answer?" he queried mockingly. "Or is that the silence of assent?"

He shifted his hand and pulled her forcefully into his arms, kissing her with a rough passion that caused the familiar melting sensation to begin in her lower body. When their lips parted, he murmured huskily,

"You'll just have to continue hating and distrusting me, Brenna, because I'm not going to let you go. I'm holding you to our bargain till hell freezes over."

"Or until you tell me to go," she said with a catch in her voice, remembering the words of their original bargain.

He bore her down on the bed, his hands and lips beginning their passionate ritual. "Yes, until I tell you to go."

TEN

"You're late, Brenna," Marcia Owens said with mock severity, her dark eyes twinkling. "That's the second time this week. Better watch it or you'll be getting a pink slip in your pay envelope." Donovan's secretary was an attractive, dark-haired paragon of efficiency. She was in her middle thirties with a wry sense of humor, and this wasn't the first time she'd teased Brenna about her dual position as Donovan's wife and unpaid help in the office.

Brenna made a face at her. "Sorry, Marcia. I wasn't feeling well this morning. I must be coming down with something. I told Michael to go on without me, but I felt better later so I came on in."

She shrugged out of her tailored peach pantsuit jacket, and hung it in the closet, placing her brown handbag on the hook beside it. "I know how much you depend on me," she added teasingly, as she strolled back over to the desk.

They exchanged smiles of complete understanding. They both knew that Brenna's presence was completely superfluous in the executive offices at Twin Pines. Marcia Owens handled Donovan's affairs with the exceptional efficiency that he demanded of all his employees. Brenna's contribution consisted of typing a few letters, occasional filing, and relieving Marcia for her coffee breaks. Nevertheless, Brenna enjoyed her mornings working in the office with Marcia. They had formed a great friendship in the last three weeks, and she had discovered a rapport with the older woman that she had found with few of her contemporaries.

The secretary shook her head ruefully. "You must be a glutton for punishment," she said lightly. "Why don't you stay home and pamper yourself? It isn't as if Mr. Donovan is cracking the whip over *your* head." Marcia Owens studied her boss's wife with envy-free admiration, thinking idly how truly lovely the girl was in the simple cream silk blouse and the peach slacks. It was true that Brenna had been of negligible help since she had volunteered her assistance, but she sincerely liked Brenna Donovan and enjoyed having her quiet, cheerful presence in the office.

It was obvious to her that Donovan felt the same way. Brenna seemed to exert a subtle, soothing influence on her employer on the mornings she was there. Though it was not in any way obvious to anyone that did not know Donovan extremely well, Marcia had worked closely with the man for some six years, and she could read the signs. She remembered how he had come out of his office yesterday, a stack of contracts in his hand. While he explained to her what he wanted done with them, his eyes were drawn, as if by a magnet, to the unobtrusive figure of his wife across the room at the filing cabinet, where she was quietly filing some papers. He had not interrupted his instructions, he had not even spoken to Brenna, but his absent gaze had not left her until he had turned to return to his office.

Brenna shrugged. "I get bored. I'm not used to being a lady of leisure. I spend the afternoons with Randy, but he doesn't really need me now that he's got Doris. And if I didn't have something constructive to do, I'd be climbing the walls."

Marcia Owens smiled sympathetically. "After the premiere of *Forgotten Moment* I don't think you'll have that problem. You'll have more offers than you can handle," she said comfortably. "I hear you're absolutely super in it."

Brenna tapped the desk lightly. "Knock on wood," she returned. "In the meantime, I'm a mere dogsbody. What challenging task do you have for me today?"

As Brenna painstakingly began to file the stack of contracts Marcia had handed her, a wry smile curved her lips at the half-truth with which she had evaded Marcia's question. How could she confess that, after three months of marriage, she was still so besottedly in love with her husband that she couldn't stand to be separated from him for an entire day? It was a phenomenon that even the most understanding modern would look upon with unabashed skepticism. As the premiere date approached, Michael had found it necessary to spend more and more time at the executive office working with publicity and distribution.

After a week of such separations, Brenna had complained of boredom, and asked with careful casualness if she could drive in with him mornings and help in the office. Donovan had accepted just as casually, and she had become a fixture in the past three weeks. It wasn't entirely satisfactory, but at least she was close to him. She could see him, exchange a quiet word, and occasionally go out to lunch if his schedule permitted. It was for this reason she had been outraged by the bout of nausea that had plagued her this morning. There was no way some pesky virus was going to cheat her out of another morning with Michael. She had stayed home two days ago, and hadn't seen Michael until he came home for dinner that night. She had been right to fight it, Brenna thought happily, for she felt quite all right now. Sheer mind over matter, she thought cheerfully. The problem was, she had grown spoiled during the past three months, she admitted sadly to herself. Though she had not had Michael entirely to herself while he continued to work at home, she had seen much more of him than was the case now.

They had spent two heavenly days on the island, and during that time Brenna had learned a great deal about herself and Michael. She had found that she had a capacity for physical passion that shocked and amazed her. In Donovan's arms, she became a pupil so eager for her lessons, that on occasion Michael would laugh with amusement and triumph, before giving her what she entreated him for. That he was pleased with her passionate nature, she knew for a certainty. He whispered it in her ear in the wild throes of lovemaking. She saw it in his eyes when she moaned with need as he brought her to the final ecstasy. As she had guessed, Donovan was an extraordinarily demanding and sensual lover, who frankly enjoyed the act of making love. He was inventive, surprising, and so skillful that she knew before she'd been in his bed a week that he had so attuned her body and sexual responses to his demands that he could arouse her body from across the room with just a look. Her face grew dreamy, as she remembered a morning last month when he had done just that.

She had been sitting in the editing room, curled up in her favorite chair in the corner of the room, when Donovan had looked up. His eyes had gone dark, as they had wandered intimately over her slim curves, lingering over the high curve of her breasts that suddenly became firm and swollen under the tailored blouse. A hot flush dyed her cheeks, and she could see the pulsebeat in Michael's temple in that moment of almost painful awareness. She never remembered what excuse Donovan had given to the two technicians he had been talking to, nor how they had gotten from the editing room to the upstairs bedroom. It had been a wild rapturous lovemaking that had left them panting and exhausted in each others arms.

Donovan had raised his head from her

breast to kiss her lips with infinite tenderness. "Remind me to declare the editing room off limits to you, love," he said huskily. "How do you expect me to get any work done, if you persist in seducing me?" Then he had yelped as she'd bitten his ear in retaliation.

In reality, no seduction was needed to tempt Donovan into her bed. He was a man who needed physical assuagement more frequently than most, and there wasn't a night that he didn't reach for her with a hunger that seemed to grow rather than diminish with the passing of time. It had filled her with relief when she realized that Donovan did not appear to be tiring of her. It had been her most persistent fear in the past months. Inexperienced though she was, she realized that men often grew bored with sexual affairs once the novelty had worn off, and Donovan's reputation for discarding mistresses frequently seemed to indicate that he grew bored more easily than most. What was sheer heaven to her, might become repetitive and dull to a man of his experience. When he had shown no signs of lessening passion, she had breathed a profound sigh of relief. She lived with the sad knowledge that Donovan did not love her, indeed, might never love her, but as long as he wanted her physically, she had a hold on his emotions and that was better than nothing. It was much better than that, Brenna thought wistfully, Donovan might not give her love, but he did give her profound physical ecstasy.

An added bonus of Donovan's knowledge of Janine's tragic story, had been a complete change in his attitude toward Randy. As he had told her, he sincerely liked children, and had a way with them that was fast making Randy his willing slave. He now often joined her in the afternoon to play with Randy and just laze by the pool in an aura of domestic contentment that filled her with a poignant wistfulness. Carefully, she did not let herself linger too long on these bittersweet memories. She must take one day at a time in a relationship such as hers with Michael, and savor each one to the utmost. Who knew how many days she had remaining? Passion without love was a reputedly unstable and ephemeral commodity.

She had finished the filing, and had turned to Marcia to request something else to do when the door to Donovan's office opened, and her husband came out accompanied by a short, gray-haired man in a rumpled brown business suit. Michael was being uncharacteristically charming for a man of his blunt, abrasive personality as he ushered the man to the front door, and Brenna wondered idly who the rather anemic-looking individual could be.

The smooth charm was gone in an instant, when he turned around and spied Brenna standing by the filing cabinet. He did not respond to her smile, as he crossed to stand before her, a frown making his roughhewn features even more intimidating. "What the hell are you doing here?" he asked bluntly. "I told you to stay in bed."

His roughness no longer phased her. "I'm much better now," she said serenely. "It's just a bug."

"I wish you'd called me," he said. "I have a date for lunch that I just can't get out of."

Brenna felt a twinge of disappointment, which she valiantly strove to hide with a smile. "No problem," she said quietly. "I'll find someone else to have lunch with." She made a face at him. "You're not irreplaceable you know, Mr. Donovan."

His eyes took on a strange stillness. "Aren't I?" he asked lightly, with a thread of underlying seriousness. "I'm beginning to think you may be, Mrs. Donovan."

He touched her lightly on the tip of her nose before turning briskly and returning to his office, leaving Brenna with a radiant face and eyes that reflected the sudden hope his light remark had given her. She firmly chastised herself for making too much of the teasing statement. He probably hadn't meant anything by it, but it was the closest he had come to admitting that there might be a future for them beyond the boundaries of a marital affair.

Her dazed eyes met the amused stare of Marcia, and she flushed with embarrassment. "Who was that funny little man with Michael?" she asked quickly, hoping to avert one of Marcia's teasing wisecracks.

Marcia raised a knowing eyebrow at the rather obvious diversion, but she answered obligingly. "Daniel Thomas; he is some sort of genius in the research department of Cinetron films. Mr. Donovan thinks he might be on the right track in developing cinematic videotape. He's been trying to persuade him to quit his job with Cinetron, and come here and concentrate his efforts solely on developing the videotape. He's having a few problems convincing him. Evidently Mr. Thomas is nearing the retirement age and has built up quite a bit of seniority with Cinetron. So far, the large monetary settlement hasn't been the persuasion that your husband thought it might be." She shrugged. "It's only a matter of time. Mr. Donovan always gets what he wants."

Brenna nodded, smiling. "That's for sure!" she said vehemently and then blushed again as Marcia broke into an irrepressible chuckle.

Brenna had no doubt that Michael would find a way to obtain the services of Daniel Thomas. She had become aware that Michael had a violent antipathy for the whole Hollywood system, where more often than not films were initiated purely on their box office potential and not on artistic merit. He, too, believed a brilliant picture deserved an equally brilliant monetary reward. But in his eyes an expertly crafted motion picture was the goal, not the tinkle of the box office cash register. Though he still had to deal with the Hollywood money men occasionally, he was gradually attempting to cut himself and Twin Pines entirely free from the system. Evidently, this little man held one of the keys that Donovan had been searching for.

At present all theatrical films had to be processed by the film laboratories in Hollywood, but Donovan was convinced that it was just a matter of time before theatrical films could be transferred to tape. Time, and research geniuses of the calibre of Daniel Thomas, Brenna corrected herself. Once such a film was developed, it would break one of the major chains that still bound Twin Pines to Hollywood. Donovan most certainly would bend every effort to winning Thomas to this purpose.

The rest of the morning passed fairly quickly, with the usual stream of visitors in and out of Donovan's office, and the light clerical duties that Marcia gave her. She had just finished typing the last page of a contract when she looked up to see Jake Dominic standing before her, looking tan and fit and incredibly handsome in white pants and a navy blue sports shirt.

"Jake!" she said delighted, jumping up and giving him both her hands in greeting. She hadn't seen him since about a week after the picture was completed. Michael had told her that immediately after a picture was finished, Dominic always set sail in his luxurious yacht, *Sea Breeze,* and was gone for an unspecified time, until he was rid of the tension of directing and grew unutterably bored and eager to return to work. That the cruise always included the presence of a beautiful and willing woman went without saying. This time Brenna had heard it rumored that his companion had been the wife of the head of state of a small South

American country, and that the State Department had been biting its collective fingernails with fear that, this time, Dominic's affair would cause an international incident.

Yet here he was, looking as casual and arrogant as ever, as he smiled down at her with that wickedly arched eyebrow. "My God, Brenna," he said teasingly. "What other uses is Michael going to find for you? Wife, mistress, actress, and now secretary. I'm going to have to whisk you away on my next cruise, just to see that you get a rest."

"From what I hear, the women you take on your cruises get considerably less rest than I do," Brenna said dryly, her eyes twinkling. "You look in reasonably good health for a man who has been reputedly dodging machetes, or is it *bolos?*"

"Neither," Dominic said lazily. "It was all much ado about nothing. The lady's husband is quite complacent as long as she handles her affairs discreetly."

Brenna giggled at the thought of a cruise with Jake Dominic being considered discreet, and a reluctant smile tugged at his lips. "I missed that laugh of yours," he said softly, and his dark eyes were suddenly tinged with a touch of loneliness. "It was a bore," he said wearily. "More so than usual."

Again Brenna felt that poignant tug of sympathy for this brilliant man who had everything a man could want, and was still jaded and even curiously lonely.

"Perhaps next time you should try a Swede," she said lightly, trying to gently nudge him out of his depression.

It worked. Dominic's mercurial temperament responded, and the black eyes gleamed mischievously. "I've already gone that route," he said with a shudder. "They're much too aggressive. I was totally exhausted by the time I got back to port."

"What about her?" Brenna asked grinning.

"Oh, Helga immediately took off for Switzerland with her ski instructor. I hear he was a candidate for the Olympics before she got her hands on him." He sighed morosely, his eyes twinkling. "He's never been heard of since!"

Brenna chuckled irrepressibly. "What are you doing back in Twin Pines?" she asked. "Michael didn't mention you were doing a picture?"

He shrugged. "I'm ready to go to work. If I have too much time on my hands, I get restless, and *voilà* — trouble."

"It seems I've heard rumors to that effect," Brenna agreed demurely. "Are you the important lunch date my husband can't break to escort his own wife?"

"Not me, sweet, but I'll act as a substitute, if you'll wait until I see that unchivalrous husband of yours," he said. "I want to pick up a script Michael told me about. Some thriller about a nuclear power plant. Michael says it has possibilities."

"Done," Brenna said cheerfully. "I'll be ready to leave when you're finished with Michael."

With a wave of his hand, Dominic entered Donovan's office without knocking, and Brenna went to the closet to get her jacket and purse. When she returned to her desk to extract the contract from her typewriter and hand it to Marcia, she was amazed to see the older woman convulsed in laughter. As Brenna stared at her blankly, the secretary wiped tears from her eyes and gasped penitently. "Sorry, Brenna, I was just eavesdropping, and it struck me as funny."

"What did?" Brenna asked, puzzled.

Marcia's eyes danced. "The calm way you accepted the foremost rake of the western world as a second-best substitute for your husband. No one would believe it."

Brenna grinned. It did seem funny when she looked at it from Marcia's point of view, and if one didn't know that the husband in question was Michael Donovan.

"If you'll forgive me for interrupting your chat, I'd like to see Mr. Donovan." The husky voice was dripping sarcasm, and they both looked up, startled, at the woman who had entered the office unnoticed. Brenna's eyes widened as she recognized the woman standing there. The large violet eyes, wild riotous ash-blond hair, and curvaceous figure were as famous as the throaty voice. Melanie St. James, who had rocketed to stardom in her first picture, a Michael Donovan production. With a pang, Brenna recalled that the gossip columns had also been filled with speculations regarding Donovan's torrid affair with his gorgeous protégée.

Marcia Owens recovered her aplomb swiftly. "Is Mr. Donovan expecting you?"

The pouting lips tightened. "Of course, he's expecting me," she said arrogantly. "We have a luncheon date."

Brenna felt a cold pain somewhere in her midriff, as she heard the woman's words. So this was Donovan's inviolate, unbreakable luncheon date, she thought numbly.

Marcia Owens shrugged, and picked up the phone. "I'll tell him you're here," she said coolly. "At the moment he's with Mr. Dominic."

"Jake Dominic?" Melanie St. James inquired, her eyes taking on an almost greedy glitter. "I've never met him. Is he working with Donovan now?"

"Occasionally," Marcia answered remotely, and spoke into the receiver. "Mr. Donovan will see you now. Miss St. James," she said as she replaced the receiver. "Go right in."

A smile of triumph lit Melanie St. James' face. "I told you he'd see me," she said with smug satisfaction. "After all, he called *me*." She swept by them and into Donovan's office, leaving Marcia Owens in an agony of sympathetic embarrassment as she carefully avoided Brenna's eyes.

Brenna said nothing as she moved toward the restroom like a sleepwalker. Refusing to think of anything at all, keeping her mind carefully blank, she washed her face and put on fresh lipstick. She tidied her hair carefully, taking as much time as possible, so that she wouldn't have to return and be present when her husband swept the voluptuous actress out of the office. She was not consciously thinking, but her instinct for self-preservation prevented her from exposing herself to that degree of torture.

When Brenna returned, Dominic was standing by Marcia Owens' desk and they stopped speaking abruptly when she entered the room. Dominic took one look at her set white face, muttered an imprecation beneath his breath, and crossed to take her by the elbow. "Dammit all, what fools you women are," he said roughly. "Come on, we're going to lunch and I'm going to try to talk some sense into you."

He half led, half propelled her from the room, and any protests she might have made were quelled by the grim stormy look on Dominic's face. This was not the same Dominic she had joked and teased with such a short time ago. She obeyed meekly as he settled her in his black Ferrari and whisked her to a small restaurant on the edge of town. It looked more like a small brick residence than a restaurant, and there was only a small sign quietly advertising quality cuisine in discreet letters.

It was only after they had been seated at a quiet corner table and Dominic had given the order for both of them, that he turned to Brenna with quiet determination in every line of his face.

"All right, now we talk," he said briskly. "Will you please tell me why you're looking like a Christian who has just been thrown to the lions?"

Trust Jake to think in such visual terms,

she thought numbly, but she had no intention of confiding in him. The wound was too raw to bear probing by that ruthless intellect. "Perhaps I'm not feeling well," she said evasively. "Marcia will tell you I was a little under the weather this morning."

"Bull!" Jake said succinctly. "We both know the reason you're falling apart at the seams. I hoped to get you to bring it out in the open yourself. But if you won't, I will."

"I don't want to talk about it," Brenna said rigidly, looking down at her folded hands on the white damask tablecloth.

"Too bad!" Jake said coldly. "Michael's my best friend, and I hope you're going to be a close second, Brenna. I'm not about to let some foolish, womanish misconception hurt either of you. Now, let's talk about that promiscuous little sex kitten Michael took out to lunch today."

Brenna flinched. "I don't see any evidence of misconception," she said with an effort. "It seems to be perfectly clear."

"It always does to a woman," Jake said dryly. "Did it ever occur to you that he could have a reason, other than the obvious one, to see the beauteous Miss St. James? They are in the same business, you know."

"She isn't under contract to Donovan any more," Brenna said miserably. "Everyone knows that she signed with Fox two years ago."

"About the same time she and Donovan called it quits," Jake observed coolly. "If I remember, it was Donovan who tired of her. So why the hell would he want to stir up the ashes of a dead love affair?" He grimaced. "Believe me, there's nothing less appetizing once you're through with a woman."

Dominic's brutal frankness was less than comforting when she realized his ruthless attitude was essentially the same as Donovan's. She shivered uncontrollably with the pain of the thought. Would Donovan some day feel the same distaste for her as he did his past mistresses? Was he, even now, trying to tell her, in this cruel and ruthless fashion that she must not count on any real permanency in their relationship?

"You're a good friend to Michael, Jake," she said huskily, her brown eyes bright with unshed tears. "But I think it's you who isn't reading the situation correctly."

"Hell!" Dominic said roughly, his black eyes worried. He covered one of her hands with his own. "Michael doesn't give a damn about Melanie," he said earnestly. "Take it from one who knows. Before you came along women were just something to use and throw away to Michael. In fifteen years, I've never seen him act the way he does about you. The man's obviously crazy about you, you little fool."

"That's comforting," she said bitterly. "Maybe I'll last a few months longer than Melanie St. James." She ran her hand through her hair wearily. "Jake, I know you're doing what you think is best, but all this discussion is tearing me to pieces." Her lips quivered uncontrollably. "I couldn't possibly eat anything. Would you please take me home?"

Jake sighed, and his face was a picture of dissatisfaction as he took some bills from his wallet and threw them on the table. "I should have known better than to try to argue with a woman where her emotions are concerned," he said gloomily, as he rose. "Come along, little martyr. I'll take you home where you can sulk, and brood, and build up a really horrendous case against Michael by the time he gets home tonight. *Women!*"

Perhaps due to this last harsh condemnation of Jake's, Brenna tried to do exactly the opposite when Dominic had dropped her off. She kept herself feverishly busy all afternoon. Playing vigorously with Randy in the pool, then cleaning out and rearranging dresser drawers in her bedroom. She tried to read a script that Michael had left for her, but this was a lost cause. Her mind refused to take in one word of the dialogue.

Michael called three times that afternoon, but she refused to speak to him, giving a vague excuse each time to the puzzled and upset Mrs. Haskins. When he made his last call, he left a message that he wouldn't be home to dinner, a message that Mrs. Haskins delivered with barely concealed, righteous satisfaction. The housekeeper adored Donovan, and she obviously thought Brenna was mistreating her idol.

Brenna herself refused dinner, and returned to her room to settle down and wait for Donovan's return. She realized at once that this was a mistake as clouds of depression rolled over her horizon, making her as brooding and self-pitying as Dominic's accusation. She jumped up, and hurried to the bathroom, filling the aqua tub with steaming, bubbling water while she bundled her hair on top of her head. She dropped her clothes carelessly on the floor and stepped into the tub, reclining full length, her head resting on the plastic pillow affixed to one end of the tub. The water was warm and soothing and like liquid silk against her flesh. Suddenly she remembered that first day on the island, and Michael beside her in that Sybarite sunken bathtub that was built for lovemaking. She could feel her nipples harden, as her mind helplessly replayed the love scene, the first of many that had gradually bound her to Michael with golden chains. She could feel the silent tears that she had fought all day long run down her cheeks in silent profusion, and she knew the time had finally come for self confrontation.

Jake had not truly realized why she had been so devastated by Michael's luncheon date with Melanie St. James. She was not foolish enough to think that Michael had finished with her yet: He was still too eager to possess her. Their lovemaking was too good for her to make that mistake. It may have been a perfectly innocent interlude as Jake had suggested. What had shaken her world to the foundation was her own reaction to that first agonizing suspicion that Donovan might be growing tired of her. The pain had been breathtaking, blacking out the joy of living as if it no longer existed. She had realized then how she had been deceiving herself.

Since she had first discovered her love for Michael, she had convinced herself that an emotion that beautiful could only enrich her, and make her stronger in the years to come. She had not realized that Michael had painted the canvas of her life with his own bright hues, and without him, all the exuberant vitality would vanish as if it had never been. Her love for him had grown with each passing day. Heaven knows what stage of dependency she would reach if she remained with him any longer. If she left now, it would be like losing a limb but she would survive. If she waited until she was discarded, as Michael had left her with no doubt she eventually would be, she was not at all sure that it wouldn't destroy her. It had been that realization that had so stunned her and left her bereft — the knowledge that she must leave Michael, and that it must be accomplished soon for self-preservation's sake. She must break her word to Michael, because she knew he was not ready to let her go yet.

The tears continued to flow and she brushed them aside impatiently. She had always had to be strong and independent. She would get over this stupid pain and weakness and emerge stronger than ever. She would leave, and never see that strong-willed Irishman again. She would make a life for herself and Randy, and it would be a good life. She closed her eyes and the maddening tears continued to flow. She would do all these things, she assured herself sadly, but first she would take one final night for herself. She would say a last "good-bye" to her love, Michael Donovan.

She got out of the tub, drying quickly, powdering liberally with her lavender-scented talc, before donning her favorite negligee set. It was a wonderfully romantic gown. Its white silk background was sprinkled with minute pink roses. The tiny sleeves, low rounded elasticized neckline, and empire waistline lent a Regency air to the ensemble. The matching peignoir was a loose drift of white chiffon with long loose sleeves. She slipped into a pair of white satin mules, and brushed her hair into a bright shining cape. She looked with bittersweet approval into the long oval mirror on the closet door. Yes, this was the image of her that she wanted Michael to hold in his memory when she was gone. She turned off the bedroom light, and left the room to go downstairs to wait for Michael.

She was curled up in one corner of the couch in the living room, idly leafing through a magazine, a little over an hour later when the front door was thrown open explosively. She could hear Donovan's rapid footsteps in the hall.

He came through the living room door like a small hurricane. He had discarded his suit jacket and was dressed in black slacks and a white shirt opened carelessly at the throat. His hair glowed brilliantly under the overhead light, and, as usual, he seemed to draw all the radiance in the room to himself. His face was taut and angry, as he crossed to the couch and pulled her roughly to her feet. "Dammit! I could beat you," he said furiously. "What the hell do you mean by refusing my phone calls? You know damn well I was tied up with appointments and couldn't come to you. I've gone through hell all afternoon, since Jake called and told me what an asinine snit you'd gotten yourself into. *Women!*" he finished disgustedly.

A little smile curved Brenna's lips. "That's what Jake said," she said, her brown eyes twinkling.

He paid no attention. His jaw was set belligerently as he continued harshly. "You're going to shut up and listen to what I have to say, dammit. I had a damn good reason for taking Melanie to lunch, and if you weren't so stubborn, I would have told you what it was when I called."

"Have you had anything to eat?" she asked quietly, her eyes running lovingly over the blunt, rough features.

"What?" he asked, caught off balance for once, blue eyes surprised.

"Did you have any dinner?" she asked.

"No, I didn't take the time," he said impatiently. "Look, Brenna, we've got to get this straightened out."

"I'll fix you an omelet," she interrupted, smiling. "You can tell me all about it while I'm cooking. The coffee is already prepared."

She wriggled out of his grasp and preceded him down the hall and into the kitchen. He followed her closely, almost as if he suspected her of trying to escape him. She gestured to the breakfast bar. "It won't be a minute," she said serenely. She poured him a cup of coffee, added the small dollop of cream he used, and stirred it briskly. She carried it carefully to the bar and set it before him.

His hand closed on hers as she released the cup, and she looked up to meet eyes that were bright with suspicion. "What game is this you're playing, Brenna?" he asked. "Jake said you were more upset than he'd ever seen you this afternoon. Yet now you're as cool as a cucumber. Don't you want to hear about Melanie?"

She returned his gaze steadily. "If you

want to tell me," she said quietly, "but it's not really necessary. Jake was right; I over-reacted."

She could feel the tension gradually leaving Donovan's body. "I'm glad you realize that," he said lightly. "I had visions of having to chase after you and drag you back by your hair."

Brenna's gaze dropped to their interlocked hands. "I'm still here," she said evasively. "Now, if you'll release me, I'll make that omelet."

His grip reluctantly relaxed, and he leaned back on the stool and idly watched her as she bustled around the kitchen, beating the eggs, adding the milk, and heating the omelet pan, before pouring in the mixture. He didn't attempt to speak until she set the savory omelet before him, poured herself a cup of coffee and perched on the stool opposite him.

He took a bite of the omelet and looked up at her. "I needed Melanie to do a favor for me," he said abruptly. His mouth twisted cynically. "Not that Melanie ever did anything for anyone without suitable compensation. This was no exception. I had to write her a very hefty check for her trouble." He was eating steadily, his eyes watching Brenna's serene face alertly for signs of distress or suspicion. "I persuaded her to try to charm someone I want to join my organization. The old man is a great fan of hers, and I thought introducing her to him might conceivably tip the scales my way."

"Daniel Thomas?" Brenna guessed.

Donovan nodded. "That's right. He joined us for lunch today."

"Did it work?" Brenna asked, sipping her coffee slowly, and idly studying the way his thick, crisp hair clung to his head like a molten cap.

Donovan shrugged. "It's too early to tell. If it doesn't, I'll try something else."

He had finished, and he pushed his plate away. He took a swallow of coffee, and his hand reached out once more to clasp hers.

"You scared the hell out of me, you know," he said quietly. "I even called Phillips and told him to report to me if you left the house."

"Poor Bob. What a skittery female he must think me," she said lightly. She returned the pressure of his hand affectionately, and then rose and reached for his plate and utensils. "I'll just rinse these and put them in the drain."

"No, leave them," he said thickly. He drew her gently around the bar, to stand before him, his eyes running over her with a look that was a long embrace. "You grow more beautiful every day, do you know that?" he said hoarsely. He reached beneath the misty robe to pull the elasticized neckline down to bare her shoulders, before putting his lips to the pulse beat in the hollow of her throat. It leapt, as it always did, at the light touch of his tongue. Her breath almost stopped, as his hands closed on her breasts and thumbed the nipples through the light silk of her gown. He, too, was breathing quickly as his lips closed on hers in a long kiss that left them both languid and hot with need.

"You'd better be upstairs and in bed in two minutes," he said raggedly, as their lips parted. "Unless you want to explore how erotic making love in a kitchen can be."

She grinned and kissed him gently. "Some other time," she promised lightly. She turned away quickly, as a swift jolt of pain went through her. There would be no other time after tonight.

She was waiting for him when he came into their bedroom a few minutes later, sitting quietly on the bed, her feet tucked beneath her. She had removed the robe and slippers, and had an air of childlike docility as he approached her.

His eyes were warm and intent on her as he started to unbutton his shirt.

"No!" she reached up and stopped him. She knelt on the bed, and her fingers replaced him at the task. "Please, I want to do it," she whispered, her doe eyes wide and pleading. "I want to do everything for you tonight. Show me how to make you happy."

She slowly unbuttoned his shirt, and slipped it from his massive shoulders, placing little gentle kisses on his chest and throat as she did so. She had spoken only the truth when she said she wanted to make him happy. Not only did she want to capture a very special memory for herself, but she wanted to give Michael the same joyous gift. Her arms slipped around his strong throat, and she kissed him gently, tenderly, with all the love she possessed for this difficult, exciting man. "Show me," she entreated quietly.

In the hours that followed he did show her what she desired. She memorized every muscle of his body as he had once done to her. She learned with lips and hands how to raise him to the height of desire and satisfaction, and in doing so, reached her own rapture. They came together not once, but many times that night. Donovan was as indefatigable and insatiable as she, as if half comprehending the desperation that drove her to pour forth her love in this the only way Michael would accept. It was shortly before dawn when Donovan fell asleep, his arm still cradling the warmth of her body.

But Brenna remained wide awake, her strained desperate eyes on the gradually lightening sky seen through the bedroom window. She knew, with a wrench that threatened to tear her soul apart, that it was time for her to go.

ELEVEN

It was a little after noon when the taxi pulled up before the Rialto theater, and the driver politely came around to open the passenger door. Brenna got out, payed the amount on the meter, and headed for the stage door with a hurried stride. It was her last step in her flight from Donovan, this meeting with Charles Wilkes, and she was anxious to get it over with.

It seemed incredible that less than eight hours ago she had been in Michael's arms, and now she was seeking Charles' help in removing her from his world permanently. The silent, almost furtive escape from Twin Pines with only an overnight case and a sleeping Randy, and the long drive to the airport in Portland seemed years, not hours ago. She had been in luck. After parking the Mercedes, and leaving the keys in an envelope addressed to Michael at the ticket counter, she had been able to get a flight down to Los Angeles within thirty minutes. She only had time to phone a very concerned and puzzled Charles Wilkes, and arrange to meet him at the theater at noon, before the flight was called.

Brenna was reluctant to ask for Wilkes' help, but she saw no other alternative. She had frighteningly little money after she had paid for the plane tickets and the taxi to Vivian Barlow's apartment to drop Randy off. She desperately needed a job and a place to stay, and it could not be in Los Angeles. She had broken her commitment to Michael, and she knew how determined and ruthless he would be in claiming what was due him. Charles had contacts with repertory troupes throughout California, as well as ties with several universities and academic establishments. If anyone could get her to a safe haven, it was her former mentor.

The stage door was open, as she expected, and she stopped a moment to smooth her hair, and tuck the melon silk blouse into her camel slacks. There was no sense in looking more disheveled and desperate than necessary. Charles was going to be concerned enough, when she asked for his help to escape from Michael. He had been almost childishly pleased when he had learned of their marriage.

She walked quickly down the shabby, dimly lit hall to Wilkes' small office. The door was slightly ajar, and she could see a small pool of light from the metallic desk lamp on the ancient pine desk. She pushed open the door.

"Come in, Brenna."

The blood drained from her face, as she stared transfixed at the red-haired man, who rose lazily to his feet at her entrance. Donovan was casually dressed, as always, in rust corduroy jeans and a cream cotton shirt that was left carelessly unbuttoned almost to his waist. He had rolled his sleeves up to the elbow.

"Michael!" Brenna said, stunned. She took an instinctive step backward, as panic urged her to flee.

"Don't even think about it," Donovan said, his voice hard as steel. "I'd catch you before you reached the stage door." His blue eyes were cold and razor sharp. "You're going to come in, and we are going to have a few words before we go on to my apartment. Do you understand?"

Brenna shook her head sadly, as the shock of his appearance dissipated. "No, Michael, I'm not coming back to you," she said quietly.

"You will," he said arrogantly. "I don't know what this is all about, but I intend to get to the bottom of it."

Brenna came a few steps into the room, her brown eyes pleading. "All the discussion in the world won't change my mind. Let me go, Michael."

A muscle twisted in Michael's jaw. "The hell I will."

Brenna sighed tiredly. After all the pain and agony of leaving him, she would have to do it all again. "Where is Charles?" she asked despondently. "Did he call you?"

Donovan shook his head. "I called him about thirty minutes after you did. When I discovered you were gone, I knew you'd run to either him or Vivian Barlow. I told him we'd had a little marital spat, and that I'd meet you in his place." His mouth twisted cynically. "He was delighted to oblige. Charles loves a happy ending."

"I'm sorry you've gone to such trouble," she said, not looking at him. "I'm afraid it was a waste of your time. Good-bye, Michael." She turned to go, but he was around the desk in seconds and grasping her arm in a clasp of steel.

"No way, Brenna," he said silkily. "You're coming with me, and we're going to talk. Because if you walk out of my life, you're going to do it alone. You're not taking Randy with you."

Her eyes flew to him incredulously. "What are you talking about? Randy's mine!"

"Possession is nine tenths of the law," he quoted ruthlessly. "And I have possession. He's on board the Lear jet right now enroute to Twin Pines with Doris Charles. Monty picked him up from Vivian's apartment five minutes after your taxi pulled away from the curb."

Brenna shook her head dazedly. "No," she said desperately. "You're lying. Vivian wouldn't give Randy to a stranger."

"You've forgotten how persuasive Monty can be," he said coolly. "And after all, he was your husband's representative." He reached behind him, and lifting the phone receiver punched a number rapidly. "Speak to her yourself," he said mockingly, offering her the receiver. Two minutes later Brenna handed the receiver back to him, her face white. "It's virtually kidnapping, you know," she said numbly. "You're as bad as Paul Chadeaux."

His face was rigid with anger, and the blue eyes flickered dangerously. "I'll let that pass for now," he said coldly. "But don't push your luck, Brenna. I'm not feeling particularly tame at the moment."

291

Neither was she. The shock and numbness was melting rapidly under mounting rage and indignation. How dare even Donovan pull something this arrogant and cruel?

"So what's the next move, Michael?" she said bitterly, her brown eyes flashing angrily. "What ransom are you asking to give me back my son?"

"At the moment, only that you accompany me to my apartment," he said. "As I said, we have some talking to do." He gestured to the door. "Shall we go?"

The taxi ride to the high-rise apartment complex was made in complete silence. Brenna's anger rose steadily as she had time to dwell on the sheer audacity of Donovan's move. It was not enough that he had all but wrecked her life and the chance of happiness with any other man, but he had to take from her the only other person she loved as well. By the time they had ridden the elevator up to the penthouse apartment, and Donovan had unlocked the door, she was almost fuming.

She swept angrily into the apartment and stomped down the thickly carpeted stairs to the sunken living room. She threw her purse on the rust modular couch, and looked around distastefully, noting the air of lush affluence. Cream carpet, expensive contemporary furnishings, and a beveled mirrored bar, all bespoke unlimited luxury and power.

"Very impressive!" she said scornfully, whirling to face him. "Rather like a set — 'movie mogul's penthouse apartment.' "

"I'll give my decorator your compliments," Donovan said, strolling toward her, narrowed blue eyes on her defiant face. "Those were my instructions exactly. I use this apartment chiefly for business meetings. I find a little healthy intimidation very beneficial."

"Is that why you brought me here?" Brenna asked bitterly. "Am I to be intimidated by the great Michael Donovan?"

Donovan's mouth tightened. "I brought you here so that you can explain why you broke your word to me and ran away. If I have to intimidate you to get an answer, then so be it." His eyes darkened broodingly. "We shared something pretty special last night, and I woke up this morning to find you'd left me, presumably for good. I want to know why? Was it Melanie St. James?"

Brenna shook her head impatiently. Her anger was inexplicably seeping away, replaced by the treacherous yearning that always beset her in Donovan's presence. "No, it wasn't Melanie," she said wearily. "I just couldn't stay any longer. Please try to understand."

Donovan's hands closed on her shoulders, his face white and set. "I *don't* understand, and I *won't* accept it! I know damn well you haven't been unhappy these last few months. Tell me why!"

Suddenly she couldn't stand it any longer. It was sheer torture being so catechized when her emotions were raw and bleeding. "What difference does it make whether it's now or later," she cried. "It was only a matter of time, anyway."

"It was time that I needed," he said grimly. "I think I know what happened. With your background, I realize how difficult it must be for you to trust yourself to a commitment to any man. I thought I was making progress, but this little incident with Melanie blew the whole thing up in my face." His mouth firmed determinedly. "Well, we'll just have to start again."

His words only added to her distress and confusion. "By holding my son hostage for my good behavior? How long do you think you can get away with that?"

His blue eyes met hers with implacable determination. "I can use it today and perhaps tomorrow. The next day I'll find another lever to keep you with me. And the

294

next day I'll find another. I'll keep on until there are no more tomorrows."

"Why?" she whispered, her gaze clinging to his, while an impossible hope stirred to life.

"Because I love you, you stupid woman," he grated between his teeth. "Because I damn well can't live without you."

Her mouth flew open, and her eyes grew round. For a moment she was unable to respond due to the sheer stunning impact of what he had said.

"I know you don't want any permanent relationship with me," he said raggedly, shaking her a little. "But dammit, I know I can make you love me in time, and I'm going to buy that time any way I can!"

She shook her head dazedly. "This doesn't make any sense," she said, bewildered. "You made it very plain that our marriage was only temporary."

"I was afraid I'd scare you off," he said bluntly. "I knew damn well what I wanted from the moment I saw you, but after I found out about your distrust of men, I knew I'd have to play down any hint of commitment." He shrugged, his expression belligerent. "Well, it's too late for that now. I intend that this particular commitment will last the rest of our lives. So get used to it, Brenna!"

Her eyes dropped, as a wave of unbelievable joy rushed through her. *Michael loved her.* Michael Donovan loved and wanted her, not for just the present but forever.

He must have misunderstood her silence for that of despondency, for his hands moved to cradle her face tenderly. "God! Give me a chance, sweetheart," he pleaded hoarsely. "I can make you happy. Just give me a chance."

Her eyes lifted to his, and all the radiance in the universe was shining from her eyes. "And you call me stupid, Michael Donovan," she said, trembling. "You're the one who is supposed to be experienced with women. Can't you tell when one green girl is mad about you?"

She flowed into his arms, and pulled his face down to hers. Michael's eyes were blank with shock, and his body was stiff and still as he looked down at her. Then her lips touched his, and he crushed her to him in a convulsive embrace that left them both glowing and breathless. Her hands moved down from his shoulders to caress the hair-roughened muscles of his chest as she spread a multitude of joyous little kisses over his jaw and chin. "Oh, Michael, I do love you so much!" she breathed. "I'll love you forever and ever, do you know that?"

A deep chuckle rumbled from the chest under her hands. "If you don't stop that, you're going to be asked to prove it," he said dryly, his blue eyes twinkling. "And as much as I lust after that luscious young body of yours, I still think we need to talk." He drew her down on the couch, and pulled her around so that she was half-sitting, half-lying in his arms. He kissed her lingeringly.

"Do we really have to talk?" Brenna asked yearningly, one finger lazily tracing the well-defined curve of his upper lip. He caught her hand and held it firmly.

"We do," he said with determination, his mouth twisting. "I want everything clear, all cards on the table. We're not going to have any more problems due to misconceptions. We've wasted too much time already."

She sighed deeply, and his gaze was drawn irresistibly to the delicious curve of her breast under the melon silk shirt. His hand reached out, as if to caress those tempting mounds before he stopped with an effort.

"I think we'd better talk very quickly," he said huskily. "Who'd ever have guessed you'd turn out to be such a passionate little witch. You're a constant temptation to me, love."

She smiled, her eyes embracing him with

such a dazzling wealth of love that he caught his breath. "Only for you," she whispered. "I only want you, Michael."

"It had better stay that way," he threatened jokingly, his hand tenderly stroking her hair. "I've been wild with jealousy since the moment we met. That actor at the theater, Paul Chadeaux, even Jake."

"Not Jake," she said unbelievingly. "You know Jake would never violate your friendship."

"With my mind, maybe, but my emotions were another matter. I know, better than most, what a rake he can be, and women fall for that devil's face of his like a ton of bricks. You wouldn't be the first to develop a passion for him without Jake even making the effort."

"Yes, he is utterly devastating," Brenna agreed teasingly. "I can't think why I prefer ugly, bad-tempered Irishmen."

"Shall I tell you," he asked mischievously, and bent to whisper in her ear.

A blush crept over her, but she met his eyes challengingly. "Promises, promises," she taunted.

"Exactly," he said succinctly, and she flushed again, her fingers playing with a button on his shirt as she avoided his eyes.

"Did you really know you loved me that

first day?" she asked curiously.

He nodded, his face suddenly serious. "It was as if the roof fell in. I didn't know what hit me. At first, I thought it was just lust, but before you left that day I knew it was a hell of a lot more than that." He closed his eyes, and said slowly, "It was tenderness, and passion, and a crazy kind of nostalgia." He opened his eyes, and they were dark with feeling. "A longing for home, and you were that home. I wanted to cherish and protect you till the day you died."

Her eyes were brimming with tears. "Yet when you offered me our bargain, you said it would only last until you grew bored and told me to go," she said.

"That meant forever, because I could never tell you to go," he said quietly.

She swallowed hard over the lump in her throat, and said lightly, "That's all very well, Donovan, but you could let a girl know."

He touched the tip of her nose lightly. "You haven't been exactly communicative yourself, brown eyes. How could I confess eternal love to you, when you didn't even trust me enough to tell me about the baby?"

"Randy?" Brenna asked, puzzled, "but you knew . . ."

"No, our baby," Donovan interrupted impatiently. "Don't you think it's time we talked about it?" He stroked the arch of her brow with a caressing finger. "Did you think there was any chance at all that I wouldn't want *your* baby?"

"Our baby?" Brenna asked blankly.

Donovan gazed at her bewildered face, and his brows arched in surprise. He gave a low whistle. "Well, I'll be damned. You didn't know." He chuckled. "Didn't they teach you where babies come from in that orphanage?"

Brenna sat bolt upright, as her mind scrambled to assimilate and correlate the evidence that substantiated Donovan's astounding statement.

"I'm going to have a baby!" she announced incredulously. "But how did you guess?"

"Hardly a guess," he said dryly, his blue eyes dancing. "If you'll recall I've had an intimate and pleasurable knowledge of that lovely body of yours for the past three months." He grinned teasingly. "Unlike you, I was anticipating just such an occurrence. In fact, I was planning on it. It was going to be one of the ties that bound you to me."

"A baby!" she hugged him ecstatically. "When?" and she started counting back mentally.

His arms went around her. "I figure about a month before the Academy Awards," he drawled. "That'll give you time to get back that sylphlike slimness, before you collect your Oscar for best supporting actress."

She ignored his gentle teasing, as she buried her face in his shoulder. "I may decide to give up acting," she said dreamily. "I may not have the time once the baby is born."

His amusement was abruptly stilled, as he pushed her away from him with a stern hand. His face was serious as he said, "Listen, Brenna, I might be a bit of a chauvinist, but I didn't get you pregnant to turn you into just another house frau. I admit my instincts are to lock you up in a harem and throw away the key, but I'm a realist. I want you to be so damn happy that you'll never *want* to leave me. You're an intelligent and gifted actress, and I want that part of you to be just as fulfilled as the wife and mother. So when the baby's born, you go back to work." He kissed her lightly. "We'll arrange things so that you can do both."

"Monty warned me that you were a slave driver," she said, smiling mistily. "He also said that it was worth it."

His hand tilted her head back. "It will be,

my love. I promise you. It will be." And his
lips closed on hers.

ABOUT THE AUTHOR

Iris Johansen, who has more than twenty-seven million copies of her books in print, has won many awards for her achievements in writing. The bestselling author of *Stalemate, Killer Dreams, Blind Alley, Firestorm, Fatal Tide, Dead Aim, Body of Lies,* and many other novels, she lives near Atlanta, Georgia, where she is currently at work on a new novel.